I0519634

A Weakness

for Chocolate

By Morgandy Caye

Published by
Sappa Creek Press

Sappa Creek Press

A Weakness for Chocolate

ISBN-13: 978-0985963903

Copyright © 2012 by Sappa Creek Press

The publisher acknowledges the copyright holder of the individual work as follows:

A WEAKESS FOR CHOCOLATE
Copyright © 2012 Morgandy Caye

This is a work of fiction. Names, characters, places and incidents are either the product of the author's imagination or are used fictitiously, and any resemblance to actual persons, living or dead, business establishments, events or locales is entirely coincidental.

Printed in U.S.A.

Prairie Stars

Fireflies flash memories of then
and now,
Drops of yellow light in a dark
prairie sky twinkle
Like stars falling too close to
earth,
Reminders of childhood,
running barefoot
through cool, summer grass.
Cupping my hands around tiny
lights
That glow between my fingers.
Gathering the fragile insects
into a mason jar
'Specially prepared with fresh
grass and holes
punched in the lid.
A prairie farm lantern on
my night stand
The soft hum of cicadas lulls
me to sleep.

Morgandy Caye
Copyright © 2006

For my husband. You give me the courage to believe in myself.

Other Titles published by Sappa Creek Press:

Follow the Creek: Poems from the Prairie

Morgandy Caye

CHAPTER ONE

Cade Lofton peered from beneath his black cowboy hat at the curvaceous blonde walking briskly down the street. He sat comfortably atop Buck as the big gelding slowly trailed three cows down an alley to a larger pen. She'd caught his attention in the café the first day he started this job, with her lush figure and snug jeans, and he'd been curious to find out more about her ever since. Other than introducing her, his boss, Lloyd Marshall, had not mentioned the young woman, and Cade didn't want to appear too interested, so he hadn't asked. So far, the only thing he knew for sure was that she was a hell of a cook!

She looked awfully young, and her eyes had met his with a refreshing openness and honesty when they'd been introduced. He told himself to stay away from her. Her obvious innocence was no match for a man with his background. Besides the fact that she was way too young, he didn't want to be the one to take away her belief that the world was good. He knew better.

He'd learned the hard way that you had to search long and far to find goodness, and even when you found it, it could slip through your fingers like fine- grained sand, gone before you knew what had happened.

Still, his eyes were drawn back to her, watching her walk with a grace and coordination that could only be seen in someone who felt comfortable in their body and in their surroundings. Even at this distance, he could see her full breasts swaying gently beneath her white tank top and he felt himself harden. Annoyed, he turned his attention back to the cattle, determined to ignore the young woman on the road.

Don't be getting yourself into any entanglements, Lofton, he told himself roughly, *the last thing you need is a straight-laced, innocent girl who thinks love means happily-ever-after.* Like any man, Cade enjoyed the company of women, but he knew where to find them; at the local watering hole. By the time the bar closed on Saturday night, he could always find a decent-looking woman whose resigned expression told him that she thought a one night stand was better than nothing; she didn't expect to hear "I love you;" and she didn't care if he got up and went home in the middle of the night.

That's the kind of woman for a man like me. Cade's inner voice sounded convincing, but like a magnet, his eyes were drawn once again to Sage, now further away. As she turned the corner at the end of the block and disappeared from sight, he was irritated by the disappointment he felt.

*   *   *   *
*

Sage Claremont's nimble fingers pressed into the soft pie dough, crimping the edges of pie after pie. Her hips swayed to the beat of a 1950's group, as her voice echoed theirs, crooning about loving feelings and long, slow kisses. Ten crimped pie shells lined her kitchen's center island, nearly covering its scarred butcher-block top. In a couple of hours, the crusts would be filled with creamy puddings topped with toasted meringue swirls. As her fingers crimped the last crust, Sage saw the little red light on the oven click off, signaling her that the temperature on the dial had been reached. Heat blasted her face when she pulled open the oven door and carefully placed four pie crusts on the rack, angling them to fit, then twisted the timer dial to the ten minute mark. She closed the oven door, wiped her hands on the white tea towel she had tied around her waist, and turned to the sink to begin washing up the dishes from her pastry-making marathon.

Strawberry blonde curls stuck to Sage's damp forehead as she worked. *I have this pie making down to an art form*, she thought, *it used to take me all day to make ten pies, and now I can do it in three and a half hours!* After six months of cooking for the local livestock market's café, Sage had refined her skills and learned what the farmers and ranchers who frequented the weekly auctions preferred to eat.

In addition to her pies, Sage made huge, gooey cinnamon rolls and hearty meat-and-potato meals featuring the beef and pork raised by local farmers. Even some of the down-town business people had begun coming to her café for lunch on Fridays. She was glad to see her clientele growing. She had taken on the job as a way to supplement her income as a freelance writer, the profession she had studied in college. After finishing her degree a year and a half ago, Sage had discovered that getting started in the writing market took time and persistence, and that the income was slow until a writer became established. Not wanting to give up her dream of making a living as a writer, Sage had taken on a part-time job to help pay the bills until she could get on her feet, and the café seemed like the perfect choice. It was only open one day a week, and other than that day, Sage could set her own work hours. It was also convenient because her little house at the edge of town was a block from the stockyards.

By 4:00 that afternoon, the pies were finished and cooling on the counter. The scent of their creamy sweetness drifted through the house. Sage cleaned up the kitchen again, then headed to her bedroom and changed into workout clothes for her daily walk. She slipped a white tank top over her head, and pulled blue knit shorts up her long legs. The last step was pulling her long, curly hair back into a ponytail. She looked forward to getting outside for some fresh air, and exercise always made her feel great. She grabbed her walking shoes and stepped out onto her wide, shady veranda. Pots of Boston ferns hung above a white Victorian railing. With a feeling of contentment, Sage sat down on the front step, slipped on her sneakers and tightened the laces. She loved her little, white house with its gingerbread trim. It had been a graduation gift from her grandmother Nina, who now lived a few blocks away in Pine Ridge Manor, the local retirement home. A quarter of land from the original farmstead would be her brother's gift upon his graduation.

Sage's grandparents had bought the house after retiring from their ranch and moving to town. It was small and cozy, just right for an older couple or a single person. A big yard surrounded the house, its perimeter lined with curving flowerbeds and well-placed shade trees. Sage inherited her Grandmother's love of gardening, and had added even more flowers and shrubs to the cottage-style landscape. A deep porch ran along two sides of the house, and like her Grandmother had done, Sage filled the space with white wicker furniture and pots filled with pink and red geraniums, colorful petunias, and trailing vines of ivy. Thick cushions in bright, colorful prints lined a white loveseat and two chairs, and a blue glass vase decorated a small wooden table sporting a bouquet of blue and pink bachelor buttons.

After college, Sage had moved to Hope, Kansas, the town where her grandmother lived, and where her father had grown up. She had visited Hope often as a child, and the little, prairie town held many happy memories for her. Family-owned stores and quaint antique shops lined its quiet main street. In general, its neighborhoods were filled with modest and well-maintained homes, neatly mowed lawns, and people who gave a friendly

wave to passersby. Like any town, it had its share of places
that weren't quite so nice, but overall it was a clean and pretty
town. Sage had never regretted her decision to move there.

Immediately, she had begun to update the little house. She
had started with a fresh paint in muted earth tones inside and a
new coat of white on the outside. She added flowery, feminine
wallpaper in her bathroom, and sheer, billowy curtains
throughout. She'd also spent considerable effort pulling up the
carpet and linoleum to expose the oak flooring that was hidden
beneath. Several of the room's wood floors had required
sanding, staining and varnishing to bring them back to their
original beauty. She'd worked like a fiend the first year, but it
had definitely been worth it!

It had been ten years since Grandpa died; Sage had visited
Grandma Nina each summer since, just as she had when her
Grandfather was still alive. Helping Nina with the flower and
vegetable gardens and enjoying long hours of "girl talk" filled
her summer break from college, and before that high school.
And now the gardens were still beautiful, tended lovingly by
Sage.

She strolled down the brick walk toward her arched front
gate, enjoying the mounds of blue and pink phlox along each
side of the walk, stopping here and there to pull a weed or
remove a spent bloom. She loved their bright color and the
fact that they bloomed profusely each May, requiring little
attention to maintain their healthy growth. Her white picket
fence was lined with flowers too. Pink and white peonies
bloomed hugely, interspersed with the graceful spikes of iris
and cheerful yellow daffodils. She left her front gate and
headed south down the paved road in front of her house. Sage
walked briskly, waving at her neighbor as she went past. Mrs.
Olaf, who was sitting on her little porch enjoying the warm,
spring afternoon smiled and waved back.

Half a block later, she reached the sale barn property, and kept walking south following the blacktopped road along the fence line. Lush cheat grass interspersed with small fireweeds and thick patches of dandelions filled the ditches. Sage noticed the newly hired cowboy herding three black cows to a pen near the barn. He looked in her direction and tipped his black cowboy hat as she walked by. Even at a distance, she could make out the muscular lines of his legs encased in snug fitting wranglers, and the broadness of his shoulders beneath his pale-blue chambray shirt. His horse's reddish coat glistened brightly in the sun as little poufs of dust rose around its hooves with each step.

Sage smiled and waved. Her heart skipped a beat thinking about how handsome he was! His name was Cade Lofton, and he'd started working at the sale barn last week as the yardman. Sage had been introduced to him at the previous week's sale. It had been his first day on the job, and he'd spent it observing how the auction was run. Sage had watched him as he ate lunch with Lloyd Marshall, the barn's owner. He was one of the most handsome men she'd ever seen. Tall and broad shouldered, with short, sable-brown hair, he exuded a quiet strength and confidence that Sage found very appealing. His chocolate brown eyes held a guarded expression, yet were keenly observant. His faded jeans fit snuggly, and a long-sleeved red shirt emphasized his athletic build. His worn, black cowboy boots and leather belt completed an outfit typical of the men who frequented the auction, typical, in fact, of the kind of men who lived around Hope, around the West.

She was glad she'd worn her new peach-colored top that day. Everyone told her peach was her best color, setting off the reddish highlights in her blonde hair and complementing her creamy complexion. The blouse's tailored styling showed off her curvy figure as well, and looked flattering tucked in to her snug fitting jeans. As a teen, Sage had deplored her voluptuous body, wishing for a model-thin figure like the beautiful women in the fashion magazines. But now, she accepted her shape and knew that beauty came in many sizes. She prided herself on being fit and healthy.

As she walked, she wondered if he was still watching her, but she didn't turn to look. Heaven forbid she should appear eager for his attention!

An hour and a half later, Sage finished her walk, having circled the perimeter of the small town. She'd driven the route with her car once to see just how far it really was, and her odometer had indicated a distance of about three and a half miles. That was just about right to give her a good workout. She walked back along the east side of the sale barn, near the front office, and was approaching the corner to her street when she heard Lloyd holler for her.

"Sage!" He yelled, "I need to talk to you about the summer schedule. Do you have a minute?"

"Sure," she called back, and reversed her direction, walking toward the office door. As she entered the brightly lit room, she stopped short when she realized Cade was sitting in the chair opposite Lloyd's desk. She smiled nervously, and he responded to her breathless hello with a nod. She hoped he couldn't tell how nervous she was around him. She took the seat next to him, as Lloyd sat down in his big leather chair behind the desk. The older man was smaller in stature than Cade, but his intelligent demeanor and neat appearance gave him an air of authority. Sage noticed his hair was graying at the temples and had been recently cut, and that as always, he was clean-shaven. His blue eyes gleamed with an excitement that Sage found curious. *He's got something up his sleeve*, Sage thought.

"I've finished with the summer schedule," Lloyd announced, "and I wanted you two to be the first to know when we'll be having sales. That way you can plan your own schedules." His eyes turned to the young woman in front of him, "Sage, I'm thinking of having a special horse sale on July second, and I'm hoping you'll be able to have the café open. I know that's not your usual day, but it should be good money."

"No problem," Sage responded, "Do you want the usual menu, or something different?"

"I was thinking maybe a hog roast, with all the fixings. I know a guy we can hire to do the meat, so you'd just be making the extras, like potato salad, baked beans, and cake, or something like that. I'll leave the specifics up to you. It will be much simpler if we only have one choice available, rather than letting people order off the menu."

"That sounds great," Sage answered, "I'll be glad to work an extra day. I can always use the cash." *Especially while I'm waiting to see if my latest article gets published,* she thought.

"I knew I could count on you," Lloyd grinned with appreciation. He been pleased with how Sage ran the café, and the quality of food was so much better since she'd taken over.

"Now, Cade," Lloyd said, redirecting his attention to the younger man, "I'll need you to take on some extra cattle duties while I am lining up the horses and buyers for the special auction. I want it to be a high-class sale, and that will take some work. I want good, sound ranch horses and high quality colts. Mainly, you'll need to ride the pastures where I have yearlings, checking the windmills and watching for any illness in the cattle. On sale days, I'll hire the day help to stay a little longer than usual, freeing up some of your time for the pasture cattle. Does that sound okay?"

"Sure boss," Cade said, thinking to himself that he'd prefer the pasture work any day. It certainly wouldn't be a hardship to spend the warm summer days riding his big, sorrel gelding, Buck, across the wide expanses of grass that covered the rolling hills of western Kansas. It beat the hell out of riding up and down the dusty alleys at the sale barn.

"Also," Lloyd spoke up, disrupting Cade's reverie; "I want to serve the food outside on the day of the horse sale. I thought maybe we'd use boards laid across sawhorses, with hay bales to sit on. You can set them up on the grass under those cottonwood trees east of the office. I'll even invite people from downtown to come out and eat. It will be good publicity. I want you two to work together on planning the outdoor set up. Sage, Cade can help you with any moving and lifting."

"Sure," Sage almost whispered, then cleared her throat and tried again, "Yeah, okay Lloyd," she finally spit out, She glanced sideways at Cade, who was staring at the floor, then looked back at Lloyd.

"I mean, if it's okay with Cade?" she added hesitantly.

Cade quickly looked up.

"I can do that," he agreed, glancing at Sage.

"Just let me know what to do and I'll be there." He almost smiled at her, she realized, then apparently thought better of it and looked back toward Lloyd.

"Well, that's all I needed then." Lloyd ended the discussion, "Thanks for coming over, Sage. You two work together on this, and I'm sure it'll be great."

Sage stood quickly and nearly ran from the room. Her heart was pounding. The idea of working closely with Cade Lofton made her excited and terrified at the same time. Just being near him in the office had left her tongue-tied. What would she be like when she had to work with him? It was too embarrassing to think about. She hurried on home, determined to get her mind back on matters at hand, namely the book she was working on. She spent the evening typing at her computer, revising the story line on the romance novel she had started several months ago, but as she worked, her mind kept drifting back to the memory of those chocolate brown eyes meeting hers, and almost smiling. She decided she had a definite weakness for chocolate!

Later that evening, as Cade Lofton sat in the living room of the trailer house that was provided for him as part of his job, he couldn't keep his mind off of Sage Claremont. Today in the office, he'd been able to smell the clean scent of her, and the fresh shampoo-smell coming from her soft reddish blonde curls. Her shirt clung to her body, damp from her recent workout, and outlined the soft, full shape of her breasts. He could swear she hadn't been wearing a bra, but he hadn't gotten a good enough look to tell for sure. He didn't want to be caught staring at her chest! Her long legs were lightly tanned from her daily walks, and her low-cut white socks made them seem even longer. He'd finally had to quit looking at her completely, before he embarrassed himself. Luckily, when she'd gotten up to leave she'd been in such a hurry that neither man had time to stand up politely as she exited. He knew if he'd stood up, the evidence of his attraction to her would have been clearly visible. Just thinking about it made him hard again. *Damn her!* He thought, even though he knew it wasn't her fault. He was pretty sure she was interested in him too. She'd been as tongue-tied as he'd felt. That was why he'd made a distinct effort to speak as little as possible while she was there.

Just great! he thought. And now he had to work with her. It was going to take all his will power to keep his hands off of her. But he knew, for both their sakes, that nothing could happen between them. He was the experienced one. He was the one who had to make sure nothing happened. As he sat in the darkened room, the light from the television casting shadows on the walls, he mind drifted again and again to Sage. If he thought hard enough, he could still smell the sweetness of her hair, still see the outline of her nipples through the tee-shirt. He knew it was going to be a long night.

CHAPTER TWO

The next morning, Sage carefully carried pies out to the trunk of her waiting car. The early morning air was still chilly at this time of year in northern Kansas, but she knew that it would warm up quickly as the day progressed, especially in the café's small kitchen. Even with air conditioning, it became unbearably hot during the midday rush. It might be chilly now, but she new her lightweight pink top would feel good in a couple of hours. On sale days, Sage pulled her hair up into a loose twist at the back of her head, allowing some soft tendrils to hang around her face. It was more sanitary that way, as well as being cooler. Nice jeans and her most comfortable cowboy boots completed her workday attire.

Twenty-minutes later, Sage had her red two-door car loaded with all the food for the café, and was on her way for the short drive to the barn. She always arrived an hour before opening in order to have the coffee ready and the cinnamon rolls warming in the oven. Although she didn't serve breakfast, the gooey rolls and freshly ground coffee were always appreciated by the farmers and ranchers who had gotten up extra early to get their stock to town for the sale.

She backed up to the café entrance, popped her trunk, and was digging through her purse for her key when she heard footsteps in the gravel beside her. She looked up, expecting to see Lloyd, but was pleasantly surprised to see Cade approaching.

"Good morning," she greeted him warmly, "you're an early riser."

"Yeah," he replied, "I came out at 6:00 to get the chores done. I was heading back home for a cup of coffee when I saw you and thought maybe you could use some help?"

"Definitely!" she responded. "It usually takes me about ten trips to get all this food carried in. Thanks for offering."

Sage unlocked the café door, dropped her key in her pocket, and pulled the door open. After flipping on the light switch, she grabbed a rock sitting outside the building and propped the door open, then turned to the trunk and retrieved two pies. Turning to Cade, she handed him the homemade pastries topped with heaps of meringue and toasted coconut.

"Just set these on the counter for now," she directed.

His stomach rumbled as he looked at the pies, and coconut was one of his favorites! He'd been going to go home and eat some breakfast after choring, but then he'd seen Sage and all thoughts of eating had left his mind. Seeing the pies had brought his hunger back with a vengeance! He deposited the pies on the green Formica-topped counter and turned as Sage walked in carrying a heavy drink cooler.

"Let me get that," he ordered, "It looks awfully heavy." He finished with a softer tone in his voice.

"Thanks," Sage gasped, "it's heavier than I thought." He took the cooler from her, his hands brushing hers as she let loose of the handles and shifted the weight of the cooler to him. With apparent ease, he carried the cooler on into the café.

"Where do you want this?" he questioned.

"On that counter behind the register," she directed, pointing to an island cabinet. It sat behind the circular counter that was lined with barstools and provided an eating spot for sale-goers. The counter took up about a third of the large room. The rest was filled with booths and tables. Old, brown carpet covered the floor. Even when clean, it wasn't what Sage considered attractive, but under the circumstances it was perfect. Even when the weather was good, a certain amount of "stuff" was tracked in, and during muddy weather, the floor was a disaster by the end of the day.

Sage headed back to the car, and by the time she'd picked up two more pies from the trunk, Cade was behind her ready for another load.

"There's a big roaster full of shredded beef in the back seat," she announced. "Just set it in the kitchen near the grill." Cade opened the door of her car, pushed the bucket seat forward, and leaned in to pick up the roaster. His senses were assailed by her scent, and his eyes took in the feminine frills she'd added to her vehicle. Her college graduation tassel hung from the rear-view mirror, and the scent of coconut filled the car, probably from one of those little bags of smelly stuff, he thought. He could never remember what they were called. Her purse sat on the passenger-side seat, and was unzipped, revealing a wallet, a checkbook, and a couple of lipsticks poked in a pocket near the side. A novel lay on the backseat floor, and the cover depicted a rugged looking pirate embracing a beautiful woman in a low-cut gown. Her breasts appeared ready to fall out of the lacy neckline. Cade wondered what Sage would look like in that dress.

"Stop it Lofton," he chided himself,"you're acting like a schoolboy."

"Can you get it?" Sage questioned.

Cade jerked back, bumping his head on the top of the car door as he lifted up the roaster.

""Yeah, I got it," he winced. He wondered how long he'd been looking inside her car; surely it had only been a few seconds. "She probably thinks you're a nutcase," he told himself as he followed Sage into the kitchen. He couldn't help noticing how her jeans hugged the rounded curves of her bottom as she walked ahead of him. He set the beef-filled roaster on the counter where she had directed.

"We're almost done," she smiled at him," only a couple more trips, thanks to you. I would have been another twenty minutes doing this alone," she finished with a grateful smile. The bright kitchen light made her hair shine, and in the close proximity of the small kitchen, Cade could see the lacy outline of her bra through the pink shirt. He felt his gut tighten, and drew his gaze back to her face.

"I'm glad I could help you," he said softly, "you shouldn't have to lift all that heavy stuff." She pushed open the swinging door into the dining area and looked over her shoulder at Cade.

"Let's finish up," she said with a grin," and I'll get the coffee started. Then we can have a warm cinnamon roll and coffee before we have to start working. How does that sound?" she asked, looking into Cade's deep brown eyes. *Or chocolate,* she thought to herself, *I could definitely go for something chocolate.*

Cade made the last two trips, carrying in the two remaining pies, and a big bowl of lettuce salad. He put the salad in the refrigerator, sat the pies on the counter, and looked up to see Sage setting two cups of steaming coffee and two warm rolls on a table near the kitchen. It smelled heavenly, and he felt his stomach growl in anticipation. As they ate, Sage found herself telling Cade about why she had come to the small community of Hope to live after finishing college. She described her summers here with her Grandparents, and how much she had loved the place. She couldn't believe she was telling him so much. He probably didn't even care, she thought. But the interested expression on his face encouraged her, and she went on to describe how her Grandmother had given her the small house, and how they were still so close. Her parents resided in Denver, the city where she'd grown up, but she'd known she didn't want to live there all her life. The small town atmosphere had seemed the perfect place to begin her writing career.

"So, you're a writer as well as a good cook?" he teased.

"I am. At least that's my dream," she finished softly. "Tell me about your dreams, Cade Lofton?" she asked quietly. She saw the guarded expression return to his eyes, and for a moment she regretted asking. But she wanted to know about this man, this quiet, handsome man who'd shown her kindness and been interested in her dreams.

I'm not ready for this, Cade thought, *I can't tell her that I lost my dreams a long time ago, that I quit trying to be something I'm not. She won't understand,* he tried to convince himself. He realized she was waiting expectantly for him to say something.

"I don't have any dreams," he said with finality. Then, draining his coffee cup, he said, "Thanks for breakfast. I better get to work." and walked out the backdoor of the café. Sage sat there in shock! She couldn't believe he'd left so abruptly. She felt stupid for telling him so much about herself. He obviously didn't want to share *his* past. She must have misread the situation. He probably thought she was one of those women who talked too much. She flushed with embarrassment when she thought back to how she had rambled on.

"What an idiot I am!" she blurted out.

"Sage?" she heard Lloyd's voice from the office, "did you say something?" he hollered.

Pushing herself back from the table, she picked up the dirty dishes, sat them on the counter, and walked to the office door.

"Just talking to myself, Lloyd," she responded. "The morning is getting on. I better get to work before the hungry hoards descend," she finished with a forced laugh.

"Got those cinnamon rolls heated up yet?" Lloyd queried.

"Sure do," Sage answered. "I'll bring you one, along with a cup of hot coffee. How would that suit you?"

"Great!" he shot back, "you're a life-saver!"

Sage spent the morning busily preparing for the hungry lunch crowd in between waiting on the early arrivals that stopped in the café for coffee while waiting for the auction to begin.

At 11:00, her first waitress, Ellie, arrived, and freed Sage up to focus on her dinner preparation in the kitchen. She loved this part of the day; pulling together all the final ingredients for the dishes she'd planned. She turned to the large stockpot on the stove. Steam from the hot, boiled potatoes filled the air, and she breathed in their starchy scent. After dropping in a stick of butter, pouring thick cream over the top, and sprinkling on a small handful of Kosher salt Sage picked up a large potato masher and went to work smashing up the mealy potatoes. Next, she skimmed the beef drippings of fat and brought them to a boil, then whisked in a water and cornstarch mixture to make a thick, rich beef gravy. One of the favorite menu items at the café was a hot beef sandwich, and many of the patrons said that Sage's gravy was the best they'd ever tasted.

All together, three women worked for Sage in the restaurant. In addition to Ellie were Helen and Shirley. All three were farm wives who enjoyed a day in town and the chance to earn a little extra pocket money. They had all worked in the café for a number of years, and their experience had been a lifesaver to Sage when she had first started. Helen and Shirley would arrive at 11:45, and only work through the

busiest time from about 12:00 to 1:15 or so. The special Sage
had planned for the day was Swiss steak, mashed potatoes,
green beans and a homemade roll. It was easy to make, well
liked, and other than the meat, the same food was served with
the roast beef dinner, so she only had to make one vegetable
and a huge pan of mashed potatoes. She had learned early on
that easy was best.

*   *   *   *   *

Cade walked into the café about 11:30, hoping to grab
lunch before the auction started. He knew if he didn't eat now
it would likely be late evening before he got another chance.
He wanted to see Sage again, too. He knew he'd been rude this
morning when he left her so abruptly, but he'd gotten scared.
He hadn't known what to say. He liked listening to her, but
when she started asking questions and the tables were turned,
he had bolted. She probably thought he was crazy! After all, it
had been a simple enough question. She wanted to know
about his life. He just wasn't sure if he wanted her to know. It
hadn't been pretty, and it had been so nice to sit there with her,
drinking coffee and listening to her talk. He hadn't wanted to
scare her off by telling her about himself. What decent woman
would want a man with his background? As soon as he walked
in the door, his eyes were drawn to Sage. He could see her
through the order window. The heat of the kitchen and the
hard work had loosened the knot in her hair. Tendrils had
escaped and curled around her face, forming a reddish halo.

"Halo is an apt description," Cade thought to himself,
"she's about as innocent as an angel." He kept looking, hoping
to catch her eye and smile, to let her know he was sorry about
how their morning breakfast had ended. He chose a stool at
the counter where he could see her as she worked. Finally,
when one of the waitresses placed an order, she glanced up.
Cade caught her eye, but her expression hardened and she

looked quickly away. He felt his stomach sink. He hadn't thought she'd be so angry about his departure that morning. He ate his hamburger and fries, methodically plowing through the food, although his appetite had left him when Sage had met his gaze. He continued watching her as he ate, but she never again looked his way.

"Order," Ellie had called, and Sage had looked up into the smiling eyes of her best waitress, and good friend. She started to smile, and then her eyes met the chocolate brown gaze of Cade Lofton. She could see the tentative smile in them, but quickly looked away. She was still mortified over her long-winded conversation this morning. She certainly wouldn't make the mistake of thinking he was interested in her again. How embarrassing! She focused her attention on Ellie again, taking the order slip from her hand.

"That new cowboy's a real babe, isn't he?" Ellie said in a whisper. "I hear he's single too."

"Really," Sage answered, trying to appear disinterested. "Well, the last thing I need right now is a man in my life. Writing and cooking for this place are all I have time for," she said, hoping she sounded convincing.

"A young thing like you needs some excitement in her life," Ellie commented. "It's no fun to work all the time!" She finished as she grabbed an order and turned to deliver it. Sage forced herself to not look in the direction where she knew Cade was sitting. Finally, after she knew he had to have left because the sale was starting, she went out front to refill her glass with iced tea. Thank God that was over. She hoped he wouldn't come in for supper after the sale. There was nowhere else to eat at that time of night. The sale usually ended around 5:00, but by the time the cattle were sorted and loaded out to the new owners, it was often 8:00 or later, depending on the size of the sale that day. Most of the help came in for a hot meal before heading home, and she expected Cade would be among the group. Oh well, she'd just stay in the kitchen and let Ellie handle the waitressing duties.

You can't hide in the kitchen forever, Sage thought, *after all, he was the rude one. So what if you misread the situation and thought he was interested. You barely know the man. How are you supposed to know what he's thinking?*

By the time the crew came in for supper, Sage had garnered the courage to help out front like usual. She could put on an act as well as anyone, she decided, and proceeded to laugh and joke with the other men just like always. Ryan, a young man hired about a month ago to run the scales, was his usual flirtatious self.

"Hey Sage," he spoke up, " you going to the dance with me tonight?" he asked teasingly. A local bar called The Watering Hole often had dances on Friday nights, the same day the cattle auctions were held. Often the sale barn crew headed out to the dance after work. Sage had been invited several times, but always had an excuse. She didn't want to give any of the guys the wrong idea. She wasn't interested in dating any of them. Her refusals had seemed to fuel the fire though, and several of the men had taken it as a challenge. Now, a Friday did not go by without at least one of them asking her to the dance. She suspected they had a wager riding on which one of them could get her to say yes to a date. She was about to respond with her usual refusal, when her eyes met Cade's. She noticed a distinct irritation in their brown depths.

You didn't want me this morning, Cade Lofton, so how dare you act irritated that someone else does. Sage thought angrily. And in the heat of the moment, she turned to Ryan and said, "Yes, Ryan. I'd love to go to the dance with you." Shocked by her response, the crew sat in stunned silence for several seconds, then Ryan blurted out a resounding "Yessss!" bringing laughter from the rest of the crew.

"I'll pick you up about 9:30," he remarked.

"Great!" Sage said, with more enthusiasm than she actually felt. *What had she let her anger get her into*, she wondered? Oh well, she just hoped it taught Cade Lofton a lesson. Someone wanted her even if he didn't.

CHAPTER THREE

After cleaning up at the café, Sage finally pulled up in front of her house about 8:30 p.m. tired and not really looking forward to her date with Ryan. He seemed like an okay guy, and he wasn't bad looking, but he'd always seemed kind of immature. Actually, he probably was a year or two younger than her twenty-four years, but normally she wouldn't have thought twice about that small an age difference. Unfortunately, his maturity level seemed not to have caught up with his actual age. She only hoped the evening was passably enjoyable.

After a short but relaxing shower Sage stood in front of her bathroom mirror and blow-dried her hair into a mass of reddish blonde curls. She applied makeup a little heavier than her usual everyday look, emphasizing her creamy complexion and long-lashed blue eyes. When she was satisfied that she looked sufficiently alluring, she went to her closet and spent several minutes surveying her wardrobe. She finally settled on a pair of white shorts and a feminine yellow top covered with tiny blue and pink flowers. She thought the colors would complement her developing tan nicely, and the pastels seemed appropriate for a warm spring evening. As a second thought, she grabbed her navy sweater. She knew that by the time she returned home it could be a bit chilly. She was just slipping on her sandal when the doorbell rang. Her stomach did little flip-flops, as she approached the door with a small amount of apprehension.

"Hey Ryan," she greeted him warmly, "come on in and I'll grab my purse and sweater." Ryan stepped into her living room and glanced around at the feminine décor.

"Nice place you've got here," he commented. But Sage couldn't detect much sincerity in his tone. She suspected the Victorian décor was too frilly for his taste. She favored lots of plants, lace curtains, and overstuffed furniture covered in floral fabrics. She found the room to be light and airy, and most of all very relaxing and peaceful. She'd always thought that how a room made you feel was the most important part of the decorating.

"Ready?" Ryan asked, after she'd grabbed her sweater, tied it around her shoulders, and picked up her purse.

"Let's go," she said, trying to interject a note of excitement into her voice. Ryan's quick glance told her she hadn't done a very good job, but he turned and led the way to his muddy green pickup truck.

"Sorry this is so dirty," he said apologetically, "if I'd known you were going to accept my offer, I would have washed it before the sale."

"It's okay, Ryan," Sage responded with a forced laugh, "as long as it gets us where we're going." She crawled into the passenger side door, and was immediately assaulted by the odor of his manure-covered boots. Apparently he'd stuck them behind the seat and forgotten to take them out when he went home to shower. She quickly rolled her window down, and acted like she didn't notice the horrible smell. They drove to the bar in silence, and as they entered, Ryan held the door open for her.

At least he's that much of a gentleman, she thought to herself, but when she remembered how helpful Cade had been that morning, Ryan's small deed paled in comparison. *Don't even think about him!* She scolded herself, *He may have been nice in the beginning, but you saw his true colors when he got up and left.* She forced a smile on her face and allowed Ryan's hand to touch her waist as he guided her through the crowded bar to a table near the dance floor where some of the other sale barn crew were seated. Several of the married men were with their wives, and Sage smiled a greeting at two of the women that she knew. They quickly introduced her to a brunette that she had not seen before. She sat next to the women, with Ryan on her left.

"What can I get you to drink, honey?" Ryan asked in a proprietary tone of voice. Sage raised her eyebrow at him for using the endearment, but he didn't seem to notice.

Oh great, she thought, *this isn't starting off well.* She hoped Ryan didn't think he owned her just because she'd accepted one date from him.

"I'll take a light beer, honey" she said in a sarcastic tone of voice. He looked at her with surprise, but didn't respond before he turned and walked toward the bar. She hoped he'd gotten the message that she didn't care to be called "honey".

"You showed him!" whispered Ann Black, the woman on Sage's right. Ann occasionally came to the auction with her husband, and Sage had become acquainted with her when the couple ate lunch in the café. "Jim and I were both surprised that you were coming here with Ryan! What's going on Sage?" Ann continued.

"I guess I had a moment of insanity," Sage said jokingly.

"I guess you did," Ann laughed. "He's an okay kid, but pretty immature for you, I'd say."

"I'll have to make the best of it," Sage replied with a smile, and as she turned to look toward the dance floor, Ryan returned with her beer. She smiled and mouthed thank you, knowing she'd have to yell to be heard over the loud music. Out of the corner of her eye, she saw Cade come in the front door. He'd cleaned up, and his rugged masculinity nearly took Sage's breath away. His dark blue jeans fitted him like a glove, emphasizing his slim waist and long, muscular legs. A white western shirt with a black yoke and black pearl snaps defined his broad shoulders. A black cowboy hat sat atop his dark hair, making his brown eyes even darker.

Like melted bittersweet chocolate, thought Sage dreamily. Reluctantly, she dragged her gaze away from him before he noticed her looking. She was through with him. He'd had his chance with her and thrown it back in her face. As Cade headed toward their table, Sage quickly turned to Ryan and asked him to dance. Luckily the band had just started on a two-step tune, a dance Sage knew she was quite good at. Ryan grabbed her hand and headed for the dance floor, just as Cade sat down at the table.

Whew, she thought, *an uncomfortable situation avoided.* Ryan slipped his arm around her waist, took her right hand in his left, and led her expertly around the floor, in a fast-paced two-step. The band led quickly into two rock songs, and Ryan and Sage stayed on the floor. They were both laughing and out of breath when they returned to the table. The cold beer tasted great and Sage decided the night was turning out better than she'd hoped. Ryan immediately drained his bottle of beer and headed to the bar for another. Sage had declined his offer of a second beer, indicating that she still had over half a bottle left. Cade was seated two chairs down on the opposite side of the table from Sage. He'd nodded a greeting when she glanced at him after returning to the table, but since then she'd determinedly avoided his gaze. She talked animatedly with the other women, and listened as Ryan told some off-color jokes that had the whole table laughing. She danced once or twice with other men that she knew from the barn, and once with Ann's husband, only after he had asked his wife's permission. They'd all laughed at that, and Sage had good-naturedly followed him onto the floor for a fast dance. By the time they returned to the table, Ryan was again at the bar for another beer. Sage couldn't remember if it was his fifth or sixth, but he was getting decidedly drunk. His jokes were becoming more risqué, and the women had looked away in embarrassment several times. When Ryan returned to the table, he asked Sage for another dance, and without really waiting for her reply, pulled her toward the dance floor. The band was gearing up for a swing dance, and as the music began, Ryan stumbled drunkenly as he tried to spin Sage around to the music. After he had nearly dropped her, and trod on her feet repeatedly, Sage was definitely not amused.

"I think you've had enough to drink, Ryan." She said angrily. "And I've had enough of you and I'm leaving."

Ryan looked stunned, and then an irritated expression formed on his face.

"You may be a looker, Sage, but you're not much fun. Just a minute while I finish my beer, and then I'll take you home." He directed, as he headed back toward the table. He didn't even turn around to see if she was following. Sage wasn't about to get in a vehicle with him now, so she turned and walked toward the exit. Her sweater was hanging on her chair, but she didn't want to go back and get it. Then everyone at the table would know there was a problem, and Sage was already embarrassed that she'd even agreed to go out with Ryan. She did not want a scene at the table to make it even worse. She knew Ann would take her home if she asked, but it was only a mile home, and she really needed the time to think. She stopped in the parking lot at Ryan's pickup, hoping it was unlocked so she could get her purse. She was in luck, and she grabbed the small leather wallet-shaped bag and slung it over her shoulder with the long strap. Hoping no one had seen her leave, she headed south along the dark edge of the parking lot and then turned east toward home. This wasn't the main route, but she didn't want Ryan to come looking for her. She just wanted to be alone. It had already been one hell of a day. She'd only gone about 100 yards when headlights indicated a vehicle was turning out of the bar parking lot and coming in her direction.

Please God, don't let it be Ryan, she prayed silently. The last thing I need now is a drunken cowboy to deal with. Honestly, he'd been so annoyed when she had chastised him,that she really doubted he would bother to come looking for her. He was probably glad she was gone. She kept walking and didn't look up as the vehicle drew alongside her. Only when it slowed down did she look over. She didn't know whether to be relieved or more worried when she saw Cade Lofton's beat up old black truck. He reached across the seat and rolled down the window.

"Hey pretty lady, need a ride," he offered in a soft voice.

"I don't know," Sage replied in a tense voice, "have you decided you want to talk to me now?" She started walking again, not waiting for an answer.

Cade watched her in the light of his truck's low beams, and thought again how beautiful she was. He pulled his truck over to the side of the road, killed the engine and lights, and got out. He had to run to catch up with her. Those long legs could cover a lot of ground, but my, oh my, were they nice to look at. He caught up to her in a few seconds, and put his hand on her arm to get her to stop. He was unprepared for the jolt of electricity that went through him when he touched her. She turned with a gasp.

"Sorry, I didn't mean to frighten you," he said softly, as if he were talking to a skittish colt. "I just need to talk to you, to apologize for this morning. You caught me off guard when you started asking questions. I just wasn't ready to tell you about my life. I didn't mean to leave so abruptly. I guess I was running away, but I didn't mean to hurt you. Please forgive me." He added quietly.

"Okay," she responded, then pulled away from his touch and walked away. He caught up again and walked beside her.

"I saw what happened with you and Ryan. I was going to offer you a ride home anyway. I didn't want you getting in a vehicle with him. He had way too much to drink. He's just a kid, but he still should know better than to treat a lady that way." Sage could hear the anger in Cade's voice, and it was comforting to have someone care how she was treated.

"I'll be having a talk with him," Cade interrupted her thoughts, anger still underlining his words.

"It's okay, Cade. I can take care of myself. I should have known better than to accept his invitation. I've been turning him down for weeks. I guess he caught me in a weak moment." She concluded. *An angry moment is more like it*, she thought to herself. She wasn't about to let Cade know he'd been the reason she had accepted a date with Ryan.

"May I please take you home," Cade asked again, "after all, it's on the way."

"I suppose," Sage conceded, "since it's on the way and all."

Cade laughed softly, and they turned back toward his truck. Since he was parked with the passenger door by the ditch, Sage crawled in the driver's side and slid across. While old, his truck was clean and well cared for. She was pleasantly surprised when he started the engine and some of her favorite music from the sixties drifted through the cab. The light scent of his aftershave reached Sage's nose, and she breathed deeply.

"Was that a sigh?" Cade asked.

Without thinking Sage replied, "No, I just love the way you smell." As soon as the words were out of her mouth, she was mortified and turned away in embarrassment. After overcoming his initial surprise at her directness, Cade was amused to see that she was blushing.

"It's okay, Sage. I'm glad you like the way I smell. I like the way you smell too. The other day in Lloyd's office, the sweet coconut smell of your hair was driving me crazy. I couldn't even think straight." Had he really said that! *Way to go Lofton,* Cade scolded himself; *you're supposed to be keeping your distance from her, not admitting how hot she makes you.*

"Really?" She said, looking at him shyly.

"Yeah, really." He heard himself respond. Those blue eyes looking at him through thick blonde lashes made all his good intentions fly out the window. He pulled up in front of Sage's little white cottage, and turned off the engine.

"Thanks for rescuing me." She spoke in a calm voice.

"I'll walk you to the house," he stated, and opened his pickup door, stepping out. Sage followed suit, and he trailed her up the walk and on to the porch. She fished her key out of her purse, unlocked the door, then turned to Cade and gave him a soft kiss on the cheek.

"Thanks," she said softly, and before he knew it, she was inside the house and the door was shut. He stood there for several seconds, remembering the feeling of her lips on his face, her full breasts brushing against his chest, and her hand on his shoulder. And her smell, oh God, her smell! That sweet coconut scent would haunt his dreams. Slowly, Cade walked back to his truck, started the engine, and drove the one block home. His place felt lonely and empty after being with Sage. He turned on the television, stripped down to his skivvies, and grabbed a beer from the fridge. Lying back on his ratty, old sofa, Cade spent another evening trying not to think about Sage, and failing miserably. Before falling asleep, he vowed to himself that he would stay away from her. He knew he would only hurt her, and he couldn't bear for that to happen.

CHAPTER FOUR

Sunday afternoon proved to be a warm one, a precursor to the hot Kansas summer that was imminent, and when Cade had awakened late that morning his bedroom already felt like an oven. He had stayed awake late the night before, into the early morning hours if truth were told, unable to sleep after dropping Sage off. In between watching mindless sitcom reruns and old detective shows, Cade had argued with himself over his attraction to the fascinating, sexy woman down the street. He was too old for her, in experience if not in years, and he definitely wasn't the settling down kind. She was the type of woman who wanted marriage and family, and in that order. She wanted a dependable, stable, hard-working man that she could count on, a man who would always be there.

Cade thought of all the times he had moved over the past twelve years, and even before that. He'd grown up in a series of foster homes after his Dad was killed in a tractor accident on the farm where he had worked. Cade's mother had run off when he was practically a baby. In fact, he couldn't even remember what she looked like, except from pictures. His Dad had always told him she was no good, and that he'd married her because she was pregnant.

Cade had been ten when his Dad was killed, and there'd been no one else, no family, for him to go to. He remembered the terror and loneliness he'd felt when the social worker had come to their home to get him after the funeral. It was only a rental house, but it was home to Cade, and the man his dad had worked for had offered to take care of selling the furniture, and finding a buyer for the old truck his dad had driven for as long as Cade could remember. He remembered when he got the check. Another social worker had showed it to him about six months later. It was only $800.00, but it had seemed like a fortune at the time. She'd helped him open a savings account, and he'd kept the money until he turned eighteen and went out on his own. It was one of the few things that had given him comfort all those years living with strangers, knowing he had that money.

During the eight years he was in the system, Cade had lived with four different families in Nebraska. Three of them had been nice, but it had never been the same as his real Dad. Even though they took good care of him, he knew they didn't really love him, not the way they loved their own kids. The fourth and last foster family had been hell. Cade was glad he'd been older, all of sixteen, by the time he got sent to them. The old man had been a drunk, and his wife, a slovenly, crabby woman, wasn't much better, even though she was sober. They obviously only took in a foster kid for the money, and they made sure they kept most of it for themselves. He'd barely had enough to eat, and his clothes had been the cheapest rags they could find at garage sales and second hand clothing stores. He could still remember the humiliation he'd felt walking into his new high school with such awful clothes. After moving so much, he was used to not really being accepted, but the clothes he was forced to wear pretty much guaranteed he'd be an outcast at that school.

The foster parents barely tolerated his presence, and were quick to criticize everything he did. After about six months, he'd gotten a job after school helping a local rancher with his horses and cattle, and had made a point of being home as little as possible. The old couple hadn't cared. If he wasn't there, he wasn't costing them anything. With his first paycheck, he bought some decent clothes and kept a stash of food hidden in his room for the nights when he went to bed hungry, which were most of them. He learned his cowboy skills from the rancher, and the man and his wife had been the best thing that had happened in Cade's young life.

When he'd turned eighteen, halfway through his senior year in high school, Cade had left the foster system and moved in to a cheap apartment. He used the money from his savings to buy a used truck, and kept working on the ranch.

The summer after he graduated, the rancher had to let him go due to low cattle prices, and Cade had left the town where he'd spent the last two years of his youth, and headed down the road. He drove as far south as his money would take him, and ended up in southwest Texas. He'd worked a ranch there for two years until he got the urge to move on, and ever since then he'd moved from job to job and town to town.

It had been twelve years now, and he'd worked in six different states. He wasn't sure what he was looking for, but he'd know when he found it. That's why nothing could happen between him and Sage. He knew he'd be moving on, he just didn't know when.

He'd finally fallen asleep about 4:30 a.m., and when he awoke the sun was high in the sky, and the trailer house was hot. He got up, opened some windows, and vowed to get the old swamp cooler up and running as soon as possible. He showered and dressed, and then after coffee and over-cooked scrambled eggs with burnt toast, he'd headed to the grocery store for his weekly shopping.

He got back home about 2:00, put away his groceries, and stripped down to his jeans, then sat down to watch a pre-season baseball game. He'd no more than gotten into the game, when a knock on the screen door startled him. The only person who'd ever come to his door was Lloyd, and that was usually when there was a problem of some sort, so as he walked to the door his mind was racing with scenarios. Were cattle out? Had a pickup broken down? Lloyd took care of chores on Sundays, which were Cade's only days off, so if anything went wrong he wouldn't know it unless Lloyd came and told him.

He opened the screen door and was surprised to see Sage standing on the rickety wood porch looking especially fetching in faded denim cut-offs and a lacy, white tank top. And boy did she fill it out!

"Hi, Cade" she said, with an expectant smile on her face. "I wanted to thank you again for bringing me home last night. It was really sweet of you to care about how Ryan treated me, and to make sure I got home okay." She paused, and when he didn't respond she continued. "I was wondering if you could come over for supper tonight, you know, as a thank you. I want to do something for you," she finished with a rush. Cade thought she acted like she'd rehearsed what to say, and was relieved to get it out.

Sage took in his appearance with definite appreciation. His faded jeans hugged his slim waist, and a band of dark hair extended upward from his jeans, spreading across his muscular chest. She noticed his nipples hardened under her gaze. He was barefoot, too, she noticed, and even his feet were sexy. Now that wasn't something she could say about very many men! She had to admit to herself that having Cade over wasn't only to say thank you. She definitely found him attractive and wanted to get to know him better.

Morgandy Caye

Cade felt Sage's eyes burning into his skin, as she looked him up and down. When she glanced back at his face, waiting for an answer to her invitation, she was flushed and her blue eyes darkened with, what? Passion? He stepped out onto the porch, letting the screen door slam behind him.

"Yeah, I guess I could come over for supper," he agreed, "but you don't have to thank me. I just did what's right, protecting a lady." He reached out and ran a finger down the side of her face. Her skin tingled and her breathing quickened. Her eyes met his and drowned in a chocolate sea as he used his finger on her chin to pull her face up to his. Their lips met, softly as first, then harder, each tasting the passion and need of the other. Sage realized her hands were on his chest, her fingers entwined in the luxurious black hair, her palms massaging his hard muscles, rubbing over his pebble-like nipples. He groaned softly and deepened the kiss, his tongue probing between her lips, his hands on her waist, then her back, pulling her closer, holding her tightly, molding her shape to his. She felt herself relax against him, give in to his demands, and surrender to his need. When he finally pulled away from her, her knees were weak and she leaned against the side of his house trying to get her bearings.

"Do you still want me to come for supper?" Cade probed, "I'm no good for you. I don't make promises. You have to know that about me. I don't want to hurt you, so maybe you'd be better off to stay away from me. I'll respect that if it's what you decide, but as long as you understand the rules, I'll come over. Just don't expect anything from me," he said with finality. Sage looked into his eyes and saw the guardedness that had replaced the passion of a few moments ago, and something in her wanted to get past that guard, to show him that maybe she was good for him.

"I still want you…I mean want to thank you," she spoke with a certain knowing confidence that scared Cade a little. She seemed to see past something in him, and he didn't like it. No one got past the wall he'd built around himself. He couldn't allow it. Everyone he'd ever loved had died or left him, and he wouldn't let it happen again. He watched as Sage walked down the steps and around the corner of his trailer, headed back to her house.

He hadn't asked her what time, so he guessed he'd go over about 6:00. It was 4:30 now, and he went in and showered again, then put on his new jeans and a clean white shirt with pearl snaps. He watched TV until it was time to go, then walked the short distance to her house.

Morgandy Caye

CHAPTER FIVE

When Sage returned home from Cade's place, she still felt breathless from his kisses. She worked quickly to put the final touches on supper so she would have time for a leisurely bath and to get ready for her guest. She checked on the marinating steaks, turning them so both sides shared equal time in the savory smelling liquid. She added a few more fresh basil leaves from her windowsill herb garden, and then placed the meat back in the refrigerator. She'd made a tossed salad with lots of vegetables and mixed greens, and right before they ate she would toss it with the special rosemary vinaigrette she had concocted. Her specialty, homemade, hot-from-the-oven oatmeal rolls, would round out the meal.

As she finished setting the table with her mismatched antique china collection, Sage couldn't help thinking back to the way Cade's mouth had felt on hers, the way he'd tasted and smelled. Still daydreaming about him, she arranged a large vase with white peonies from her yard, and set it to the back of the table near the wall.

"Everything looks perfect," she thought, and walked down the hallway toward her bedroom, pulling her shirt over her head as she went. She turned on the water in her huge old tub, and poured vanilla-scented crystals into the water, and then inhaled deeply. She loved the relaxing aroma of vanilla. She finished undressing, dumped her clothes into the hamper, and then lit several candles on the vanity before selecting a classical station on her internet radio. With the relaxing music for a backdrop, she slid into the hot, fragrant, water and sighed deeply as she sank up to her neck.

Twenty minutes later, with the water decidedly cooler, Sage washed her hair, and then stepped out of the tub and grabbed a huge, fluffy, white towel from the rack. She dried off, then wrapped the towel around her head and walked into her bedroom. As she passed the large mirror above her dresser, she paused to assess the body she had been blessed, or cursed, with. She wasn't sure which was a better description. A shape that was definitely voluptuous reflected back at her. Her brisk daily walks and hours spent in the garden gave her a firm and toned appearance, but she certainly wasn't model material. She'd always wanted a thin, svelte shape to go along with her height, but the Claremont women were all larger than what most people considered fashionable. Still, all in all, her body didn't look too bad. Her pale creamy skin was lightly tanned from her hours outdoors, and her full breasts were firm above a flat belly and long trim legs.

"I might not be petite," Sage murmured with consideration, "but I don't need to hide in shame either. Cade seemed to find me attractive earlier this afternoon, if his kiss was any indication, and I definitely felt a sign of arousal under those faded jeans." Sage smiled knowingly to herself, then turned to the dresser to select her clothes for the evening ahead. She wanted to look nice, but not like she'd tried too hard to impress him; pretty, but not overly dressed up; sexy, but not slutty. What a dilemma. She sorted through her closet, choosing and then discarding one outfit after another. She tried on a pair of white shorts, and then decided her tan wasn't dark enough for them yet. She finally settled on a soft denim skirt with a white lace tank under a sleeveless pink blouse. She tied the blouse at her waist, and then she slipped white mules onto her feet. The shoes boasted two-inch heels, but with Cade's height, she wouldn't be towering over him. She studied herself in the mirror and was satisfied with her reflection. Just the right touch of casualness and sexiness, she decided. She felt comfortable and attractive. She sprayed on her favorite vanilla perfume, then unwrapped the towel from her head and went back to the bathroom to finish her hair and makeup. After combing the tangles from her hair, she used her fingers to scrunch it into loose curls, and then she blow-dried it with her diffuser. She applied makeup lightly, her complexion needing little enhancement. Mainly she focused on her eyes, bringing out their size and color with subtle shading and shadow. Finally, happy with her appearance, she went back to the kitchen. She had just opened a bottle of wine when the doorbell rang, and her heart was suddenly racing. She could see Cade through the screen, and the breeze blowing in carried his special scent, clean and masculine, to her nostrils.

She smiled shyly, and saw Cade's eyes darken in appreciation.

"Come in," she invited.

Cade stepped over the thresh-hold, trying to collect his thoughts enough to say something halfway intelligent. She got more beautiful and sexy every time he saw her. My God! Her legs looked a mile long in that short skirt. And he was sure he could detect a hint of cleavage through the lace top.

Say something, Lofton, he told himself, *You're being rude!* He took in her living room in a glance.

"This place looks just like you," he observed, "I mean, just like I thought your home would look." He corrected himself, feeling stupid. *Great, Lofton*, he continued his inner dialogue, *I bet she's real glad she had a sputtering fool like you over for dinner.*

Sage watched him redden, and then laughed quietly.

"It's okay," she confessed. "I'm nervous, too." A look of relief crossed his face, and Sage continued. "Come on into the kitchen. I just opened a bottle of wine. I hope you like it. I wasn't sure what kind you'd like, so I got a red to go with the steak." Cade had no idea what wine went with what, and beer was his usual choice of beverage, but he could tell Sage had tried really hard to make everything special.

"I'm sure that'll be great," he reassured, and then took the long stemmed glass she offered him. He watched her as she swirled the deep, red liquid, then tipped the glass to her lips and sipped the wine. His stomach tightened as he stared at the tiny drop of wine on her bottom lip. It tightened even more when her pink tongue darted out to lick it off.

"So, what do you think?" she questioned," Is the wine okay?" Cade quickly took a sip, and then nodded. "Let's go out on the patio," she suggested, then turned and led Cade across the kitchen and out an old-fashioned, wood-framed screen door into her secluded back yard. Lilac bushes surrounded a grassy area along her property line, and a circular flowerbed filled the center of the small yard. Water trickling from the tummy of a cherub completed the tranquil scene. Irises and jonquils bloomed profusely in the bed surrounding the cherub, and peonies lined the rear wall of the house. White, rattan furniture sported cushions covered in soft floral fabric.

Sage took Cade's hand and led him to a love seat facing the fountain.

"I love it out here," she confided. "It's my favorite place in the world."

"I can see why," Cade said, looking around appreciatively. "Did you do all this yourself?" he asked, with wonder in his voice. He didn't know much about gardening, but he was sure this would all take a lot of work.

"Some of it," she answered. "I put in the center flowerbed and the fountain, but the rest Grandma and I did over the years when I came to visit her here. She planned a project every summer. I guess I inherited her green thumb," she said laughing. Cade took her hand and peered closely at her thumbs.

"They don't look green to me," he said in a teasing voice. "But your yard is really magnificent!" Sage couldn't have been more pleased with his compliment. Turning to face him on the seat, she leaned over and kissed him on the cheek.

"That's one of the nicest things you could have said to me," she told him. They sat in the privacy of her yard, talking and getting to know each other until the sun dropped down low on the horizon.

"I better get the steaks on before it gets dark," Sage announced. "I can't guarantee how they'll be cooked if I can't see what I'm doing." She stood and walked over to her grill, filled it from a bag of charcoal sitting nearby, then struck wooden match against its box and watched the flames take off on the pre-treated coals. She looked back to see Cade staring at her, his expression unreadable.

"What are you thinking?" she asked, a friendly tone in her voice.

"I'm thinking this seems like a fairytale. I'm afraid any minute I'll wake up and be back in that old trailer house all alone." He tried to keep his voice light, but Sage could sense the undertone of seriousness, even as he tried to hide it. He laughed to cover his discomfort.

"Is there anything I can help you with?" he asked hopefully, wanting to get passed the moment of feeling uncomfortable.

"You can help me bring out the steaks and stuff," she offered, and turned to open the door. They went into the cheery kitchen, and Cade was again impressed with the homey feeling and comfortableness of her house. It was warm and welcoming, the kind of place he'd dreamed of as a kid. The kind of place none of his foster homes had ever been.

After a wonderful meal, they sat in her living room, talking like old friends. Both had slipped off their shoes, and they sat on the old over-stuffed sofa with their feet on the scarred coffee table. After a while, in a moment of comfortable silence, Cade slipped his arm around Sage and pulled her close. She leaned warmly into his side and laid her head on his shoulder. He couldn't remember ever feeling more content than at this moment.

"This has been a wonderful. Thank you, Sage," he began, "and I'm sorry if I seemed too pushy this afternoon. I just don't want to hurt you. I need you to know what I'm like and where I'm coming from." She could sense his guard coming back, the openness he'd shown all evening disappearing, and she wasn't ready for that yet.

"You didn't seem pushy," she interjected. "I'm glad you're up front with me. I like knowing where I stand. I wanted you to kiss me. I've wanted it ever since I first saw you. If you don't want a commitment, that's okay. I'm not sure I do either. But I definitely want to explore the things you make me feel."

With that, she turned and slid her hand behind his head, pulling his mouth to hers. He moaned, and returned the kiss, deepening it as their mouths opened and tongues intertwined. He leaned back against the arm of the sofa and pulled her on to him, making the kiss go on and on, molding her shape to his, running his hands over her back and down to her bottom. She could feel his growing arousal, and knew her own need was growing just as quickly. She broke away from his mouth and began to nuzzle and nibble at his ear and neck. She heard his breathing quicken, and her own responded. They rolled over on the wide sofa seat, and lay side-by-side, kissing and tasting. She slowly unsnapped his shirt, while his hands untied her blouse at her waist, and worked her tank loose from the waistband of her skirt. As she ran her hands over his chest, marveling again at the muscular planes and smooth skin, dusted with soft black hair, his own hands explored the velvety skin of her stomach and back, slowly working upward until they brushed the undersides of her lace covered breasts. He seemed afraid to go too fast with her, and finally, Sage became impatient. She sat up, pulling her blouse and tank off. Cade's gaze was fixed on her full breasts that appeared ready to spill out of the low-cut white bra. Her pink areolas were visible through the sheer lace, and her hard nipples gave away her arousal. The color of Cade's eyes reminded Sage of hot fudge, their intensity melting her like the vanilla ice cream in a hot fudge sundae. She lay back down, facing him, and pulled open his shirt, pressing her lace-covered breasts against the dark skin of his chest.

"You'd better be careful, Sage." He said with a deep groan, "You may be asking for more than you realize."

"But Cade," she said softly, "I want to know what it's all like, and I want you to teach me."

"Teach you?!" he started, a note of alarm sounding in his voice. "You mean you haven't done this before?"

"No," she admitted, "Is something wrong with that?"

"I guess not," he conceded, "but I sure had the impression that you knew what you were doing."

"Well, I've read a lot of books," she grinned, "And after all, with the society we live in, you can learn a lot about sex from watching television."

"Television!" Cade said, with exasperation. "You really are innocent," he decided. "And I'm not the one to teach you. That should be for your husband to do."

"That's so old-fashioned," Sage giggled. "I haven't been saving myself for marriage. I just never found a man I wanted to make love with until now." She wiggled against him, and the feel of her firm, lace-covered breasts nearly did Cade in. "Just one little lesson, please?" she pleaded. She saw the need and wavering resolve in his eyes, pressed her lips to his mouth, and she had him. She moved against him, deepening the kiss. With one hand around her back, holding her to him, the other had found its way to her breast, squeezing and cupping the large mound. He could feel her turgid nipple against his palm, and he rubbed gently, eliciting a moan from deep in her throat. He felt the hook at the front of her bra, and with a press of his finger it snapped open, her breasts spilling out against his chest and into his hand. He couldn't believe how lush and full they were. God, she was perfect, he thought. He wanted to see them better. He sat up, pulling her up with him, and held her facing him on his lap. The position gave him full access to her delicious breasts, and he took advantage of his position, enjoying the dreamy expression of arousal on her face as he plucked at her sensitive nipples. Just then, headlights flashed through her front window, and they heard a vehicle door slam. Sage leaped off the couch, grabbed her top, and ran for the bedroom. Cade sat there, dazed, only coming to his senses when a knock sounded at her door. He pushed himself up from the sofa just as Sage appeared, fully dressed, from the bedroom and quickly opened the door.

Lloyd stood there, a slightly embarrassed look on his face.

"Sorry to bother you kids," he said regretfully, "but I got a call about some cattle being out on the highway north of town and I'm afraid I'll need some help." He finished, looking toward Cade questioningly.

"No problem, boss," Cade responded, grabbing his hat. "It's a good thing I told you where I'd be!" Lloyd nodded, and then turned and walked to his pickup. Cade looked at Sage as he reached for the door handle. She looked so disappointed, and leaving her was one of the hardest things he'd ever done.

"If you get the cattle in quickly, maybe you can come back?" she said hopefully.

"Yeah, maybe." He replied and walked out the door.

CHAPTER SIX

Sage waited for him, reading a magazine until after 10:00, and finally realized he wasn't coming back. She tried not to feel disappointed in the way the evening had ended. She took some comfort in knowing he hadn't wanted to leave any more than she'd wanted him to go. Things had been going so fast between them. Maybe it was just as well Lloyd had interrupted. Although that idea only occurred to her the next morning after she'd had some time to collect her thoughts.

After sleeping in and eating a leisurely breakfast, Sage slipped into a summery, pink sundress paired with low-heeled sandals and headed for the retirement center to pick up Grandma Nina. Their weekly trip to church was something they both looked forward to, and had become a tradition since Sage moved to Hope. Part of the tradition included going back to Sage's house for lunch and a visit in the garden. Sometimes, when Nina felt up to it, they even did some gardening or weeding, just like old times.

On this day, with the church service behind them, the two women sat at the white, wrought iron table under the cherry tree in a corner of Sage's back yard. The tree was loaded with growing cherries, and insects buzzed among the thick leaves with a low hum that provided a natural background harmony to their conversation. Both wore expressions of satisfaction as they sat in comfortable silence. A buzzing bumblebee meandered from flower to flower, drinking in the sweet nectar from the centers of the colorful blooms. The remains of their outdoor lunch still lay on the table. A blue crock bowl contained all that was left of Sage's favorite chicken salad recipe. She always used fresh red grapes and real cream cheese, which made it wonderful and richly sweet. She'd served it on a bed of fresh lettuce picked from her vegetable garden. They'd also feasted on blueberry muffins and steamed asparagus. Nina had declared it a perfect spring lunch menu. Neither of them was in any hurry to move from their relaxed positions in the cushioned, white iron chairs.

"How is your book coming?" Nina asked with interest. She was the one with whom Sage shared ideas for her writing, and also one of the few people Sage felt comfortable being critiqued by. Before her retirement, Nina had taught English at Hope High School, and was in fact a writer herself. While she had never made a living from her writing, she had been good enough to have several pieces published over the years, and still enjoyed putting a story on paper. She had been thrilled when Sage had chosen a career path so close to that of her own. Nina had always felt she and her granddaughter were soul mates. They shared so many interests, and despite their age difference, always enjoyed each other and felt comfortable with one another.

"Oh, it's coming." Sage said with satisfaction. "Sometimes the progress seems slow, but on other days I might get ten or twenty pages done. You know how that goes." Grandma Nina was so easy to talk to, to be with. She always knew what Sage meant, and she never judged or lectured. Sage knew there had been times when Nina felt she was making a mistake, but she always let Sage make her own decisions, right or wrong, and Sage appreciated that.

"I know exactly what you mean," Nina laughed. "Writing can be compared to a river; sometimes a flood others a drought, or occasionally just a trickle."

"Good metaphor," Sage grinned.

"How are things at the sale barn?" Nina questioned. "Several people at church have commented on how good your food is. It sounds like things are picking up."

"They really are." Sage replied. "The last few weeks I've had to bake more pies, and the specials seem to go better every week. If the trend keeps on, I may need to hire another waitress to help out over the noon rush."

"That's great!" Nina responded, with pleasure in her voice. Her pride in Sage's ability and accomplishments knew no bounds.

"It sounds like the summer sale schedule will be busier than I expected, too" Sage continued. "Lloyd told me this week that he's planning a special horse sale in July, and he wants me to cook for it. We had a meeting about it this week."

"Sounds interesting," Nina mused, "what's on the menu?"

"Lloyd wants to have a hog roast. He says he knows someone he can hire to cook the meat. Then I'd only be responsible for the side dishes and dessert." Sage explained. "He wants to have it all outside, like a picnic. We're going to set up wood planks on sawhorses for tables, and hay bales will be the chairs."

"That'll be a lot of work," Nina exclaimed. "I hope he doesn't expect you to do it all yourself!" She thought she might have to have a talk with Lloyd herself if he was expecting too much of her granddaughter.

"Oh no," Sage said with a laugh. "The new yard man will be helping with the set up and all. His name is Cade Lofton, and we're working on it together."

"I didn't realize Lloyd had hired a new yard man." Nina stated. "When did the previous guy leave? Wasn't his name Dan Leahy?"

"Yes, it was Dan." Sage answered. "He left about two months ago. It took Lloyd a while to replace him. Cade only started about three weeks ago."

"Cade is it?" Nina asked. "On a first name basis, are you?" She said with a grin.

"Oh Grandma," Sage said, and felt herself blushing, "He's a really nice guy, and he seems like quite a gentleman." She told Nina about how he'd helped her carry in the food for the sale last week, and also how he'd given her a lift home Friday night.

Nina made no reply. She only observed Sage's face when she talked about Cade Lofton, noting the animation and pleasure that emerged as she described Cade.

I'm glad she's finally met someone who makes her feel alive, Nina thought. *It's about time she learns what it's really like to be in love, instead of just writing about it.* She smiled softly to herself.

"So Sage, are there any weeds that need pulling today? I'm feeling pretty spry, and I wouldn't mind getting my hands in the dirt!" Nina changed the subject, and stood up, scanning the garden with a practiced eye. She was so pleased with what Sage had done with the place since she moved in. So many wonderful things that she herself had been too old and tired to tackle alone had been easy work for Sage, and Nina was glad to have been included in the planning, and asked to help in whatever way she was able.

Lazily, Sage got up, stretched, and walked toward the peony bed.

"We could do some deadheading over here." She suggested to Nina, who promptly headed for the shed to get the garden shears and a basket to hold the spent blooms.

The women worked at a leisurely pace for nearly an hour, sometimes visiting and other times working in a companionable silence. Finally, when they'd gone around the perimeter of the back yard, Sage suggested they head in to the kitchen for a piece of the fudgy chocolate brownies she'd made that morning. Nina agreed, feeling pleasantly tired and ready for a break. They stepped into the kitchen, and both sighed at the refreshing coolness emanating from the ceiling fan whirring overhead. Nina pulled out a chair at the square oak table, and watched as Sage made two glasses of iced tea. She brought a frosty glass to her grandmother, then got out two white china dessert plates and set about cutting the dessert. Just as she was ready to scoop the sweets onto the waiting plates, a knock sounded at the door.

"I'll get it." Nina announced, "You go ahead with that." She said as she walked into the living room and toward the open front door. Through the screen, Nina spotted a handsome young man, cowboy hat in hand, looking surprised to see an old lady answering the door.

"Hello," she said cheerfully, "I'm Nina Claremont, Sage's grandmother."

"Oh", the man responded uncomfortably, "Is Sage here?"

"She sure is." Nina replied. "And who might I tell her is calling?" She wondered if this might be the new yardman she'd heard about this afternoon.

"Sorry, didn't mean to be rude," Cade said apologetically. "I wasn't expecting someone else to answer the door. I'm Cade Lofton. I work for Lloyd at the sale barn."

"Hi, Cade," Nina responded warmly, and offered her hand. He shook it gently.

"Why don't you come in and join us?" she invited. "We're just getting ready for dessert, and Sage makes a wicked brownie!" She finished with a chuckle.

"So far, everything I've tasted that Sage cooked is pretty darn good!" Cade offered, and followed Nina through to the kitchen at the rear of the house. When he entered the kitchen, Sage had her back to him. She still wore the floral print sundress she'd put on for church, but she was barefoot and her hair was loose, and curled damply around her face from the exertion of gardening. Cade's breath caught in his throat when she turned and met his gaze. Heat flared in her eyes, making them sparkle like sapphires under a tropical sun. She seemed to see through him, into him, to places he didn't want anyone to see. But for the life of him, he couldn't stop her.

At the silence, Nina turned, and when she saw their gazes intently locked she smiled in delight.

It's a love affair in the making if I ever saw one! She thought happily.

The three ate their dessert and drank their tea, chatting amicably, and Nina, ever observant, watched for clues about Cade Lofton. On the surface, he was certainly the gentleman, and definitely good looking, but Nina found she had trouble reading him. He wouldn't meet her gaze for very long, but in the brief moments their eyes locked, she could see in the brown depths of his, a shield; a wall, blocking her out. *What was he hiding?* she wondered. She didn't sense that it was anything terrible, but he was definitely hiding something. *It's funny the things people think they have to hide,* Nina mused. Maybe Sage could unlock the door to whatever part of himself was behind that wall, and Nina only hoped that if she did, it wouldn't be Sage's heart that was broken in the end.

CHAPTER SEVEN

The air conditioner whirred in the background, an unplanned accompaniment to the relaxing notes of a Mozart piano concerto floating from the stereo as Sage's fingers raced across the keyboard. She sat on an overstuffed chaise in the corner of her bedroom, her laptop propped on her knees as she wrote. She often completely lost track of time when she was writing, so she was surprised when her cell phone rang and she saw on its little screen that it was 2:15 p.m.! She had worked right through lunch and didn't even realize it.

"Hello?" Sage spoke into the pink phone.

"Hey Sage," the deep timbre of Cade's voice filled her ears. "Whatcha doin?"

"Working," Sage laughed softly. "You?"

"Unfortunately, the same," he replied. "Lloyd and I are eating a late lunch, and then heading back out to the pasture again. We're at the Dairy King right now."

"Mmmm," Sage responded, her mouth watering. "I didn't eat lunch yet, and I'm imagining a burger and fries. Is that what you ordered?"

"You're a good guesser as well as being beautiful," Cade laughed. "So anyway, the reason I called, well, one of the reasons, is that Charlie and Anne are having a dance at the Legion Saturday to celebrate their twenty-fifth wedding anniversary. I wondered if you'd like to go?"

"I'm already planning to go," she teased, "Anne invited me at the sale a couple weeks ago."

"I mean go with me, naughty woman," Cade laughed, and felt his face flush. It had been a long time since he'd been around a woman who made him get his words tangled up like a figure eight in his lariat.

Cade laughed again, "You'd better not already have a date," he teased back. *Or maybe it would be better if you did, he thought, better for both of us in the long run.*

"No," she admitted. "I was planning to go alone and sit at the old maids table! I'd love to go with you."

He laughed at her self-deprecation, "A beautiful woman like you wouldn't be sitting with the "old maids" for long."

Sage only chuckled.

"Anyway, great," the excitement was apparent in his voice. "See you then." *Geez, Lofton, the voice in his head drowned out her goodbye, you sound like a teenager asking a girl out for the first time! Get a grip!*

"Bye," Sage smiled as she closed her phone.

Two hours later, Sage closed her laptop, set it on the floor next to the chaise, and stretched. She was now officially starving! She'd completed the general plot of her book several weeks ago, and was editing and revising her story now. While she enjoyed all aspects of writing, the revisions were really her favorite. She loved thinking of more descriptive words that painted a picture in the reader's mind, and ways to develop her characters that made them seem real.

This was actually the second book she had written; the first was a short, romance novel she'd done while still a student in college. Even though at the time she thought it was a great book, she'd had no luck getting it published, and when she'd read her story a couple of years later, she'd realized the problems with it. She valued it as a learning experience, and worked even harder to improve her skills as a writer.

Sage's rumbling stomach had her heading for the kitchen, where she pulled some sliced turkey breast from the fridge, along with slices of smoked provolone, tomatoes and spinach. She took two slices from a loaf of seven-grain bread sitting on the counter, spread them with mayo, and then built her sandwich. The fresh, yeasty smell of the bread along with the red intensity of the garden-ripened tomato had Sage's stomach growling even more. She also halved and cored a crisp Jonathon apple, filled the centers with chunky peanut butter, and added the fruit to her plate.

Carrying an icy glass of fresh-brewed green tea, along with her plate, Sage walked into her living room and plopped down on the sofa. She picked up the remote and clicked on the set, then scrolled to her favorite cooking channel to watch for new recipe ideas while she ate her late lunch. She wondered if there was a word for a combined lunch/dinner like the word brunch for breakfast and lunch. Drunch or linner didn't sounds too appetizing, she decided.

It wasn't long until her thoughts turned to Cade's phone call. It had been cute how nervous he sounded when he asked her out, she thought. She was pleased that he seemed to be opening up more all the time. Still she felt nervous about the whole situation, mainly because she could see herself really falling for him. She had to keep in mind that he'd told her up front that he wasn't the type for a committed relationship. Even though his recent actions didn't seem to reflect that, Sage knew she had to protect herself. She didn't want a broken heart!

Cade and Lloyd pulled in to the sale barn parking lot that evening about seven o'clock. Dust devils stirred up by the trailer's tires danced behind the rig, and followed them to their parking place near the tack barn. The two men unloaded their sweaty horses from the stock trailer and led the weary animals to a nearby corral where a tank of fresh water awaited.

After currying and feeding his horse and putting away his saddle and equipment, Cade said goodnight to Lloyd and headed for home. He was tired and hungry, and all he could think of was a hot shower, followed by food and crashing on the sofa in front of the TV. An hour later, just before he drifted off to sleep with a rerun of <u>Law and Order</u> droning in the background, Sage flashed through his mind. Cade smiled as his eyes closed, and he looked forward to the day after tomorrow when he'd get to see her again.

Saturday morning, after a disappointing survey of her closet, Sage decided a shopping trip was in order. She grabbed her purse and headed out the door for the half hour drive North to Fuller, KS. Fuller boasted a number of women's clothing stores and she spent several fruitful hours trying on tops and pants, skirts and dresses, and even several pairs of shoes. She finally found an outfit that was perfect for the anniversary dance that night. Her next stop was at a nearby gift shop to purchase a small anniversary gift for Charlie and Anne. After perusing the selection at the store, she finally settled on a set of four stone coasters with a picture of a saddle and lariat on each. She thought the coasters would fit perfectly

57

in the couple's ranch home. After a relaxing lunch of ham and tomato on toasted focaccia in a little coffee shop, Sage drove home arriving just in time to begin her preparation for her date with Cade.

Lloyd and his wife were also going to the anniversary dance, so to Cade's relief they called it a day earlier than usual. He was home and in the shower by 5:30. Before showering, he'd given Sage a quick call, asking her if she'd like to grab a pizza for supper before heading to the dance. She had agreed, although when he said he'd be over to get her about 6:30, she got a little freaked! "

There's no way I can be ready that fast, she'd moaned.

"I have faith in you," he'd teased her, and they both laughed as they hung up their phones.

So much for a long relaxing bath, Sage thought as she pulled her clothes off. *A quick shower will have to do.* The quick shower turned into a 10 minute one when she decided she had to shave her legs since she was wearing a dress tonight. Stubble wouldn't do! After drying off, Sage slathered herself with her favorite vanilla-scented lotion, and applied pink polish to her toe nails. She had just inserted her second earring when a knock sounded at the door. Grabbing her robe, Sage hurried out to the living room, and was a bit dismayed to see Cade already standing there. He was ten minutes early for heaven's sake!

"It isn't 6:30 yet," she chastised him with a smile when she pulled the door open.

"I see my faith in you was misplaced," he grinned. "But I'm not sure that's a bad thing."

Sage reddened when she watched Cade's gaze drop to her short robe, then move downward. Glancing down at herself, she realized the robe didn't leave much to the imagination. She was embarrassed to feel her nipples harden into stiff peaks under his gaze. She took a step back.

"You can wait out here while I finish getting ready." Her throat felt almost too tight to speak.

"But what if I want to help you?" He took a step toward her. He didn't seem nervous at all, Sage noted. In fact, those dark chocolate eyes were soft, meltingly so, like the feeling she got in the pit of her stomach when he looked at her.

"Somehow, I don't think your help would hurry things along," she laughed nervously.

"If I were helping you, hurrying wouldn't be our goal," his eyes were fixed on her breasts, their fullness pushing against the silky lavender fabric of her robe in a very inviting manner. The robe's tie had loosened, and the inner curves of her breast mounds peeked out from the deep vee where the robe's edges met, while her straining nipples seemed to beg for attention. Cade couldn't resist their calling. He lifted his eyes to Sage's and held her gaze while he reached up and let his thumb lightly caress one turgid point. Sage gasped, but didn't pull back. His hand moved to the other nipple, giving it the same treatment, and he saw the silver sparks of passion rising in her blue eyes.

"How am I supposed to think about pizza, when all I want to taste is you?" he whispered. Sage moaned softly in response as his fingers worked their magic teasing her sensitive buds.

"Go put on something sexy for me, sweet woman," his voice was low and deep. "When I make love to you for the first time, it's going to be slow and sweet and last all night. Now go get dressed before I change my mind," he kissed her softly, then pushed her gently toward her bedroom.

Sage turned and hurried down the hallway, her brain fogged with need. She pulled the door shut behind her, and let her robe slide to the floor. After slipping on the lacy new under-things she had purchased on her shopping trip, Sage stopped to admire herself in her dresser mirror. The sheer pink fabric of the bra and panties left little to the imagination. She imagined Cade's eyes when he looked at her, when he saw the dark pink of her aureoles and the shadow of reddish curls at the juncture of her thighs. She day-dreamed about his brown eyes darkening with need until they were almost black. Cade's voice brought her back to the present.

"You have five minutes to be out here or I'm coming in to help you."

"I'm almost ready!" Cade smiled when he heard the nervousness in her voice. He loved the way her body responded to him, but he knew it made her a little nervous. She wasn't used to how intense her body's needs could be, and even though he knew it was wrong, he couldn't wait to be the one to teach her all about it.

Sage slipped the new sundress over her head, and felt its soft, clingy fabric slide over her body. She loved the light blue color and empire waist. It was a bit shorter than she was used to, only about mid-thigh length, *but after all*, she told herself, *it is summer!* The criss-cross front displayed just the right amount of cleavage, which her new bra enhanced perfectly. She was pleased with how the dress's color was enhanced by her light tan. She slid her feet into sandals with low, kitten heels and then walked into her little bathroom for a quick application of makeup. She swept her hair up into a loose twist, and walked out of the bathroom just as her bedroom door opened.

"Need any help?" Cade's voice preceded him into the room. "Oh, I guess not," he murmured after he stepped into the room. "I can see I'm going to have the most beautiful, sexy date at the party," he reached for her hand. "Shall we?"

Taking his hand, Sage smiled and led the way out to his waiting pickup. The party turned out to be great, and Cade the most attentive and fun date she had ever had. He guided her around the dance floor in the Texas Two Step, then kicked it up for a jitterbug. She spent much of the evening laughing and breathless, and if she hadn't been tired, she would have hated to see the party end. She rode home with her head on his shoulder and soft music floating from the truck's speakers. He drove slowly, taking the back streets to her house, and stopping twice to give her soft, wet kisses and whisper naughty things in her ear.

They sat in her porch swing and talked and kissed, and caressed, until Sage's shoulder straps hung down her arms, and her lips were swollen and moist.

"Please come in with me," she asked, then moaned as Cade's big hand cupped her breast through the sheer material of her bra and massaged gently, "Please, I need you."

"Oh yes," his voice sounded hoarse and deep, "I'm coming in. You don't know yet what it means to need me." Sage could only whimper as his mouth closed over hers once again.

With her senses drugged by Cade's mouth and hands, Sage followed him to her bedroom. He sat on her bed, guided her to stand in front of him, and lifted her dress over her head. Despite her arousal, Sage felt herself blushing.

"You're so beautiful!" Cade's eyes worshipped her body, and she forced herself to keep her arms at her side. She felt her breasts and nipples swell, as if begging for his attention, and warmth grew between her legs. He reached out and softly ran his hands from her waist down to her hips, then leaned forward and begin kissing her breasts through her bra. She felt her knees weaken as the heat of his breath and the moistness of his tongue penetrated the fabric and caressed her flesh. He alternated sucking her swollen nipples into his mouth through the wet fabric as he slid the shoulder straps down her arms, and then used his teeth to pull each bra cup down until her full, firm breasts were uncovered. His eyes, dark chocolate with passion, stared hotly at her chest until Sage pulled him to her nipples again, needing his hot mouth on the sensitive peaks. He gave her what she needed as his hand roamed over her soft skin. He cupped her bottom and pulled her closer, then began trailing soft kisses down her stomach. He slid her pink panties down her thighs, and she stepped out of them. He moaned when the reddish triangle of her pussy came into view. As she stepped out of her panties, Cade couldn't resist sliding his fingers along the pink lips feeling the moistness that seeped from between them.

He stood and quickly pulled his clothes off, watching Sage's eyes as she took in his muscular physique. Her eyes widened when his erect cock was freed from the confines of his jeans, and Cade found himself even more aroused by her reaction. After rolling on a condom, he lay back on the bed and pulled Sage down on top of him. She lowered her mouth to his, her lips warm and moist as they lightly caressed his, her pink tongue darting out, tasting his lips and dancing with his tongue. Cade groaned again and pulled Sage's mouth more tightly to his own, taking ownership of her senses. She whimpered as he pulled her tongue into his mouth and sucked it gently while his hands grasped her bottom and held her tightly against his erection.

Sage felt the heat and hardness of his need pressing against her belly and pussy mound, she felt her breasts, heavy with desire, compressed between their bodies. Without thought, she began arching her hips, began rubbing against his erection with the same slow rhythm that he was using on her mouth. He alternated between sucking her tongue, and pushing his own inside her mouth, mimicking the feeling of his cock pushing against the swollen wetness between her legs.

Sage opened her thighs until her knees rested on either side of him. She felt his hands massaging the globes of her ass, pulling them apart and then pushing them together, holding her against his hardness. She felt the shaft of his cock separating her pussy lips, and she couldn't resist sliding forward, rubbing her wet slit up and down his shaft. She felt Cade's groan in her mouth. Sage sat up, astride her lover, and he cupped her breasts as she continued to slide forward and back along his swollen cock, her thick nipples caught between his squeezing fingers.

"Oh God, baby," Cade whispered, "you're so beautiful and hot! I need you, need to be inside you,"

"Yes, please," Sage heard herself whimper, didn't recognize the hot need in her own voice.

Cade pulled her down to him, and then held her as they rolled over so he was on top. She felt his weight and strength envelope her, and he kissed her softly while he reached down and guided his cock to her opening. She felt its engorged head push into the mouth of her sex, felt it begin to stretch her open. He stopped then, letting her adjust to his size before gradually pushing more and more of his cock inside her. Finally, with one hard push, his cock was embedded deeply within her. She gasped, and he stopped, holding and kissing her as the sharp pain slowly dissipated.

"Okay, baby?" He spoke softly, his mouth nearly touching hers.

"Oh yes," she whispered. "You feel so huge inside me."

"Your pussy feels like a tight, silky sheath massaging my cock. I'm going to start moving now, going to give you the hot loving that we both need."

And she felt him pull back, almost removing his cock completely before pushing forward again and filling her with his hardness. Sage moaned softly with each stroke, her pleasure growing as her swollen clitoris rubbed against Cade each time he pushed his erection into her wet heat. His pace increased and she arched her back, pushing herself onto him and against him as her body begged for release. Faster and harder he pumped in and out of her, and the smells and sounds of their arousal filled the room. Her senses overwhelmed, Sage exploded in an intense orgasm. She moaned and whimpered loudly as her pussy contracted rhythmically around Cade's cock. He groaned and drove against her once, then twice, and a third time as he came, the condom tip filling with his warm, creamy semen.

After their breathing calmed, he rolled to her side and held her close, nuzzling her hair.

"Thank you, baby." Cade kissed her softly. "It means a lot to me that I'm your first lover."

"I'm glad it was you," Sage whispered.

CHAPTER EIGHT

A warm summer sun heated Sage's shoulders as she worked quietly in the flowerbed on the east side of her front porch two mornings after the anniversary dance. Using her small pruning shears, she efficiently deadheaded and trimmed back the spring-flowering bulbs to make way for the next wave of blooming plants. She kneeled in front of the bed, leaning across to reach those plants needing pruned near the back of the bed. Her fair complexion was turning to a sun-kissed golden color under the early summer sun. Even though it was only 9:00 a.m., the hot sun promised a scorching afternoon. Sage planned to be working at her computer inside her air-conditioned house before that happened.

Cade rode up to Sage's front gate, and sat on his horse, quietly appreciating the view she unknowingly offered. Her gorgeous round bottom was barely covered by faded denim shorts whose frayed ends tickled her smooth thighs. The bottoms of her bare feet looked pink and soft as she leaned forward onto her hands to reach a plant further back with her shears. Her back was naked except for a thin black strap across the center. "Wow," Cade thought. He had to stop and think about what he'd come over for.

"Hey, gorgeous," he called in greeting. Sage whipped around, then smiled and waved. She gracefully stood up, and picked her way barefoot across the yard. Cade stepped down from Buck to meet her at the gate. Her black bikini top strained in its effort to contain her full breasts. He didn't notice her smile of welcome since he couldn't seem to look away from her chest. Her soft giggle got his attention, and he blushed.

"Hi, cowboy," she said in a soft, sexy voice. "To what do I owe the honor of this visit?" He looked at her blankly for a second, and then he blushed again. He hadn't been this tongue-tied since he was a kid. But man did she look hot!

"Well," he stammered," I was wondering if you'd want to have supper with me tonight, you know, at my place. I thought I could order a pizza or something." Sage was pleased at the effect her body was having on him. She glanced down at the noticeable bulge in his worn jeans, and then she gave him a knowing smile.

"Is eating the only thing you want to do with me?" she asked teasingly.

The little minx, Cade thought, *she's not the only one that can play this game, although she's damn good at it.* Cade slipped his arm around her waist and pulled her against him.

"We could just forget the pizza, and I'll have you for the main course." He suggested, "How does that sound?" She pressed herself into him, and he leaned down for a kiss. He felt Sage catch her breath, and a whimper escaped her delicious lips. He cupped the heavy fullness of a breast, and she breathlessly accepted his offer for supper, between the drugging kisses.

I'll show her what it means to be teased, Cade thought, and then he realized he was tormenting himself just as much. He groaned deep in his throat as her hips began rubbing against him. *Luckily we're hidden by these lilac bushes,* Cade thought with relief, *otherwise the neighbors would be getting quite a show.*

Between periods of drugged insanity brought on by Cade's hands and mouth, she realized the cups of her bikini top had slid to the sides, leaving her breasts exposed, uncovered right out in her yard in broad daylight, but Cades big rough hands rolling her sensitive nipples quelled any embarrassment. She felt her hips rubbing against him in the same rhythm he was pulling on the tips of her breasts. She'd never felt so aroused! *My God,* Sage thought, *sex is awesome, I can't believe I waited so long to do it.* But her rational mind knew that no other man had made her feel the way Cade did. He wasn't the first man to kiss her, or even to enjoy her breasts, but he was definitely the first one that made her forget where she was.

Somewhere in the back of her mind, she heard Buck stomp his foot and snort softly. Cade's hand left her breasts, but his mouth continued with its hot wet kisses. Sage realized he was tying Buck to the fence. Finally, with both hands free, he untied the bow that held the top around her neck, leaving the top dangling around her waist, and then unbuttoned her shorts and slipped a hand down the front. She hadn't bothered with panties that morning, and his fingers easily found the tangled wetness between her thighs. She moaned and rubbed against his hand, desperately needing his touch. He guided her further back inside the yard and more behind the huge lilac bushes, then pushed her shorts down over her hips so they slipped to the ground.

Cade stepped back and looked at her voluptuous body while he continued to slide his finger back and forth between her swollen sex lips. Her green eyes were half closed and dark with passion, and tiny whimpers slipped from her well-kissed mouth. He turned her around and his hands guided her into a kneeling position on the soft cool grass. He wanted to see her naked in the same position she'd been in when he rode up and saw her working in her flower bed, and he wasn't disappointed. Her full, firm bottom was tempting beyond belief, and her heavy breasts dangled beneath her like ripe fruit, ready to be devoured.

He quickly unsnapped his shirt and unhooked his belt buckle before opening his jeans and lifting his thick erection from the confines of his shorts. He kneeled behind Sage, using his knees to push her legs farther apart, and then leaned over her to cup the weight of her hanging breasts in his hands. The tip of his stiff penis rubbed tantalizingly against the wet heat of her. Sage began to rub her bottom against him, and Cade grabbed her hips and stilled them. He didn't want this to end too soon, and he was barely in control the way it was.

Cade turned and lay down on his back, his head between Sage's spread legs, and pulled her aching, swollen pussy down to his mouth. At the first feel of his tongue, she startled and tried to pull away, but Cade held her hips tightly and his hot sucking mouth soon made her forget her embarrassment. He buried his face in her musky wet heat and tasted every part of her, and when he could tell she was in a frenzy of arousal, he suckled her stiff clitoris until she bucked against his mouth in orgasm. While the waves of pleasure still washed over her, he slid up beneath her, brought her panting mouth to his, and after rolling on a condom, he guided her wetness down to his penis. He lifted his erection up so the tip of it was at her hot, slick opening, then gently began to work it ever so slightly in and out.

"Oh, God Cade," she whispered," that feels so good."

"Baby, you don't know how good." Cade responded, working himself into her a little further with each thrust. Her tightness overwhelmed him and Cade stopped moving and held her, impaled on his arousal. When she relaxed again, he lifted her up so she sat astride him, and let her body adjust to his thickness and length. He gently fondled her breasts, and after several minutes her own arousal began building again. When she seemed ready, he reached down with one hand and began rubbing her clitoris. She slowly began to wiggle up and down on his cock, straining against his fingers. He pulled her forward so her nipples were near his face, and began sucking them, first one and then the other, all the while holding her hips in a position that allowed him to work his cock in a gentle pumping motion. She quickly reached a frenzy of arousal again, and he quickened his pace, ramming his hardness into her until they both came explosively.

They lay quietly for a while, enjoying the closeness, sharing soft kisses, and gentle caresses.

"I'd better get to work," Cade finally said with disappointment. "I don't want Lloyd coming to look for me. I should be done working by 5:30 or so. Why don't you come over about 6:00 and we'll get something to eat." He finished, and then quickly sucked both of her nipples into hardness, "Or I could just eat you some more." He said with a teasing grin. Sage blushed, like the inexperienced lover she was.

"I'll be there," she said with a shy smile. Cade stood up and began to fasten his clothing. Sage started to rise and reach for her clothes.

"Don't get dressed until after I'm gone," he asked her softly. "I want to remember you like this all day." The look in her eyes told him she would honor his wish, and Cade looked at her appreciatively as he finished dressing. He grabbed her hand and pulled her around the bush near the gate where his horse was tied. She tried to pull back, afraid someone would come by and see her standing there naked, but he asked again, "Please, just for me." And she couldn't refuse.

He rode slowly away, looking at her the whole time, and she made herself stand there, exposed, for him. She felt wetness running down the insides of her thighs. When he was out of sight, she grabbed her shorts and top and ran into the house. Much to her surprise, she felt sexually aroused again, even after their lovemaking, and realized it had started when he'd asked her to remain naked while he dressed, while he stared at her, and while she stood naked in her front yard where anyone passing by could have seen her. The feeling made her long for tonight when Cade's hands and mouth would tease her and satisfy her again.

Sage spent the afternoon at her computer as planned, but as she wrote, she found her story becoming much too sexual. In fact, much to her annoyance, some of it was downright pornographic! After having to rewrite nearly a whole chapter, she gave up and spent the next couple of hours cleaning out her kitchen cabinets, then went to the store to get a supply of fresh produce. The grocery delivery truck came to Hope on Mondays and Thursdays, and Sage made a special effort to go and buy her fruits and vegetables on those days. Her small-town grocery didn't have the best selection of produce anyway, so she at least wanted to get there before it was picked over.

It was nearly five o'clock when she returned home, and the cool rush of the air conditioning hitting her face when she walked in the door caused her to breathe deeply of the drier air. Kansas could be so humid in the summer, much worse than where she'd gown up near the Colorado Mountains. She quickly washed and bagged her vegetables and fruit, put them in the fridge, then hopped into a cool shower to get ready for her supper with Cade. She'd tried to keep herself busy all day, to keep her mind off him, but it hadn't worked very well. *I can't believe I couldn't even work because I was so distracted by that man!* She chastised herself. *This is ridiculous!* Sage had always prided herself on being an independent woman, a woman who didn't swoon over men and lose her head in moments of passion. She'd always thought women who did that were silly and spineless, certainly not educated professionals like herself. She simply had to get a grip. Sure Cade Lofton was drop-dead gorgeous, sure he made her heart pound and her common sense fly out the window, but really, she was an adult, a mature woman who should be able to handle a good looking guy. It was simple really, tonight she would keep her wits about her. She certainly wasn't going to let a handsome cowboy make her forget herself.

After the talking-to she'd given herself, Sage felt empowered and ready to continue her relationship with Cade, only on her own terms this time. She dressed sensibly in tailored navy shorts that reached midway down her thighs, a white cotton blouse with short sleeves, white flowers embroidered on the front, and a demure round collar, and her best sneakers. She felt very no-nonsense and in control. She French-braided her hair into one long braid that hung down her back, sprayed on a sporty perfume, applied some light makeup and at precisely five minutes before 6:00, she walked out her front door and down the block.

Sage knocked on Cade's front door at exactly 6:00. She'd always prided herself on punctuality. After several minutes, Cade answered, dripping wet and with a thin green towel wrapped around his waist. Sage had been planning to say hello in a casual and friendly way, but the sight of him through the screen door, nearly naked with rivulets of water running down his muscular torso left her speechless.

"Hey, Sage," he said in greeting. "You caught me in the shower. Lloyd and I didn't get in until about ten minutes ago, so I'm not quite ready yet. Sorry." He finished apologetically.

"It's okay," she felt herself stammering. "I don't mind waiting."

Get a hold of yourself, her inner voice scolded. You've certainly seen him in less than a towel. *Remember, you're not one of those silly women who get all flustered around a good-looking man.* She took a deep breath and walked past him into the living room. The clean smell of him filled her nostrils, and the water on his dark skin brought to mind melting milk chocolate. Her mouth watered and she could almost taste him. He shut the door behind her, and when she turned around and met his gaze, every sensible thought left her head and she nearly swooned when his mouth met hers.

"I had a hell of a time working today," Cade said when their kiss finally ended. "All I could think about was you, and how hot and sweet you were this morning. My jeans felt damned uncomfortable several times, and I could tell Lloyd thought I wasn't paying attention."

"Me too," Sage confessed. "I tried to work on my book, but I kept thinking about you and some of the things I wrote were way too graphic for my story!" she finished with a laugh.

"I'm glad you feel the same way," Cade replied. "I hurried like hell to get back here and see you." He finished with another kiss to her soft, full lips. "By the way," he added. "You look especially fetching tonight, like a demure librarian. But I know better. I know what a hot body you're trying to hide under those conservative clothes. I also know that it's not working." He held her at arm's length, his hands on her waist, taking in her appearance. "Those shorts fit just right. They show off your sexy bottom to perfection, and I can see a hint of your lace bra through the material of your blouse, just enough to be sexy and make me want to see more."

Sage's eyes glazed over with passion as he described her attire, and a little voice in the back of her head whispered that her ploy to stay in control wasn't working, but Cade's deep warm voice easily drowned out that little whisper. He gave her a quick, hard kiss, and then released her. She stumbled forward in a daze of arousal, catching herself quickly as she turned to watch him walk toward his bedroom.

"Let me get some clothes on and we'll go get something to eat. I'm starved. We were getting in a sick steer in a pasture twenty miles from town around noon today, and we didn't have time to come in for lunch."

Sage sat down on the couch and took a deep breath. *So much for being in control!* The voice in her head came back with a vengeance. She listened for several minutes while drawers slammed and hangers clanged, and soon Cade appeared dressed in faded, but clean jeans, a white t-shirt, and his good boots. He picked up his black Stetson, grabbed his checkbook from the table, and opened the door with a flourish.

"Let's go pretty lady," he invited in a voice like warm honey, and Sage's control went out the window once again.

CHAPTER NINE

Cade walked out the door behind Sage, gazing appreciatively at her long, toned legs and firm backside, and put his hand on her waist as they walked to his pickup. He opened the passenger door for her, and after seeing her comfortably seated, he walked around and got in the driver's seat. The old pickup's finely tuned engine purred to life on the first turn of the ignition, and Cade flipped the radio dial to an oldies station, then turned to Sage.

"I thought we'd go to the Legion Club," he suggested. "They have their hamburger fry on Monday nights and it's usually pretty good. Does that sound okay?"

"Sounds great," Sage agreed. "I'm starving!" Cade noticed the look in her eyes when she glanced over at him, and his heart flip-flopped in his chest. She looked all calf-eyed. *Oh, great,* he thought. *She promised me this would just be casual. I hope that look wasn't what I thought.* He kept his eyes on the road as he drove across town and turned east on Oak Street, then pulled in to the parking lot at the Club. His inner voice was working overtime, and he gave himself a good talking to as they walked to the front door of the bar and restaurant. *You knew better than this, Lofton,* he scolded himself, *You better end this before it goes any further. She's not the type for casual sex, even though she said that's all she wanted. You* knew *it wasn't and you went for her anyway. She's way too good for a no-account cowboy like you!* Cade shuddered, and then followed Sage into the cool interior of the bar.

      Sage grabbed his hand and pulled him toward a booth in the back, and they slid in on opposite sides of the table. She grinned at him, but a smidgen of doubt crossed her face when she saw a guarded expression in his eyes. *What's going on?* she asked herself. She quickly picked up a menu and began scanning the entrees. Cade followed suit, and they sat in silence until the waitress arrived at their table.

      "Hey Chloe," Cade flirted. "You're looking real fine this evening, as always." Chloe was a woman of about fifty, with flaming red hair that had been teased and sprayed into a big 'do that not even a stiff breeze could muss. Her heavily made-up face framed friendly blue eyes that sparkled with mischief. She was a fixture at the Legion Club, having waited tables there since her divorce nearly fifteen years ago.

      "You look pretty fine yourself, Cowboy," she came back. "And I see you got yourself a pretty young thing tonight." Turning to Sage, she continued, "You watch yourself with him, Sage Claremont. He's got too much charm for his own good, and those brown eyes can melt a girl's heart" she finished with a laugh. Sage and Cade chuckled along with her, and Sage thought to herself how right the older woman was. They placed their orders, with Sage opting for the grilled chicken salad with dressing on the side, and Cade ordering the half-pound burger and curly fries. They both requested beer, and Chloe soon brought icy mugs to the table along with bottles of the chilled ale.

      Cade took a long swallow of the cold beer, then turned to Sage with the guarded look gone from his eyes. She felt herself relax a little, but she still wondered what had brought on that look. It scared her, especially after what they'd shared that morning. But she also remembered how skittish he'd been in the beginning and how he'd told her he wasn't interested in a serious relationship. *I've got to keep things light*, she reminded herself. *I don't want to scare him away.*

"So," Cade began. "Tell me more about yourself. You haven't told me much about when you were a little kid." He prompted her with a grin.

"Okay," she responded. "But remember, fair is fair. You haven't told me anything about when you were a kid!" She saw a shadow in his eyes, but it was gone momentarily, and he quickly started asking her about her youth. She'd had such an idyllic childhood, and had so many wonderful memories to share, that with little prompting from him she talked until their food arrived. They dug right in, both being famished, and not much was said until their plates were nearly empty. They ordered another beer, and he asked her more questions, focusing on her parents and siblings. She described her parents as being a happily married couple, and told him about how her dad had started his own veterinary practice and her mom ran the business end of the operation for him. She talked about how her grandparents had dreamed of her father coming back to Hope to start his practice, but that he'd preferred working with the small animals so had opted for the city. Her younger brother, Nathan, was in vet school right now, and hoped to join his dad's practice upon graduation.

After finishing their second beer, they left the restaurant and drove back across town to Cade's place. Cruising down the quiet streets of Hope, they commented on the lushness of the freshly mown lawns and the profusion of flowers and blooming shrubs that edged many of the yards in the little town. When they turned and crossed the train tracks then pulled in to the dusty expanse of the stockyard parking lot, it was a definite contrast to the landscaped yards they had just passed. While well-maintained, the sale barn facilities looked utilitarian. The barn itself, a large red-brick building was surrounded by a vast dirt parking lot that sported a few hardy weeds that had managed to persevere despite their weekly trouncing by truck and trailer wheels. The pens were mainly constructed of pipe welded at the joints and painted white, although the white paint had quickly taken on the hues of deposits left by the animals that inhabited the corrals each week.

Further back from the main barn, a couple of small, white buildings sat near the outer corrals and loading chutes. One was used for veterinarian procedures on the animals being sold, and the other housed the saddles and other equipment used for the horses whose job it was to help manage the animals that were auctioned each week. Cade slowly motored across the rutted parking lot, and pulled up to his home. The trailer where he lived sat along the edge of the auction market property, and was surrounded by buffalo grass and a few cottonwood trees, whose shade made the small, metal-covered dwelling bearable in the heat of summer. They climbed from the old, black truck and walked companionably into the house. Once inside, Sage reminded him that it was his turn to tell about himself.

"Well, there's not really much to tell," he started, obviously uncomfortable. "My growing up sure wasn't like yours. My mom left when I was real little, and Dad raised me till I was ten years old. He was killed in a tractor accident. He worked all his life as a hired hand on a farm. After the accident, I went into the foster care system. I didn't have any other family to take care of me. I lived with different people over the years, wherever the social worker could find a place for me. Not many people want a teenage boy, too much trouble, I guess." They sat on the old sofa as he talked, and she held his hand, feeling the tension in his body.

"That must have been really scary," she observed. "I can't imagine having to move in with people I didn't know when I was a kid!"

"It was," he admitted, glad that she understood. It felt good to talk about it with someone who cared. He'd spent most of his adult life avoiding the topic of his childhood. He feared seeing the pity in people's eyes when they learned of his past, and didn't want anyone to perceive it as a weakness.

Before she could ask any more questions, he kissed her, light little kisses that teased her lips like the find mist of a tropical shower, and then deepened until she forgot what she wanted to know about him; until his touch and smell and taste filled an emptiness she didn't know was there. The little voice in her head whispered, *He's doing this on purpose. He's not comfortable telling me more about himself.* She gently pushed him away, her hands on his broad chest. She smiled gently up at him, and saw the passion in his eyes as he focused on her moist, swollen mouth, then drug his gaze to her eyes. "Where did you go to high school?" She inquired.

"I went to a couple of different high schools," he replied, and then started with the kisses again, his hands softly massaging her back as he pulled her against him.

"No more kissing until you tell me as much about yourself as what I told you about my life!" she smiled, gently chastising him. "You may be a charmer, but you can't make me forget that I haven't heard much about you yet." Cade took that as a challenge. He did start talking, and with no more kisses, but his hands began to roam. He pulled her around so she straddled his lap, her knees on either side of his hips. While he talked, his fingers softly traced the outline of her lace bra through the blouse. Her nipples stiffened in response, drawing his attention. And while he continued to reminisce he rubbed the pads of his fingers across the sensitized tips of her breasts until she had trouble listening to him. He kept talking while he unbuttoned her blouse and released the front hook of her bra. He told her about his high school classes while he kneaded her firm breasts and plucked at her protruding nipples until she began to moan and rub herself against him. He finally stopped talking and took her thick nipples into his mouth, suckling them rhythmically as she held his head pressed against her breast. He worked loose the fastening of her shorts and she stood up and wiggled out of them.

She stood before him completely naked and vulnerable, and she felt intensely aroused. She started to get back on his lap, but he told her to stay where she was.

"You're so beautiful, Sage. Just let me look at you. Your body was made for sex," he crooned softly. He leaned forward and began caressing her, making her crazy with lust, making her beg to be taken, and finally when she thought she would die for wanting him, he pulled her onto his lap and filled her completely with his condom-sheathed hardness. She couldn't believe what he made her feel, and despite her soreness from the morning, she reached her peak quickly. Not long after, he followed, pumping his essence into her.

Eventually, they made their way to his bed. Its soft, rumpled sheets smelled of his clean skin, and Sage slept soundly nestled in a cocoon of warmth with Cade's arm around her waist. His big hand cupped her breast protectively and his chest pressed against her back. She woke to the sensation of his erection pressing against her bottom, but his slow, easy breathing told her he still slept. She sighed contentedly, thinking about their night together, and how happy she felt. She knew Cade was still holding something back from her about his past, but she felt they were getting closer and that their relationship was growing. After several minutes, she slipped out of bed and grabbed one of Cade's clean shirts from his closet before heading to the bathroom for a shower.

Cade's bathroom was definitely a bachelor's. While it was clean and orderly, nothing decorated the walls. His toothbrush and a nearly used-up tube of toothpaste rested on the vanity next to a small black comb, a stick of deodorant, and a bottle of Stetson cologne. She carefully unscrewed the lid to the cologne and inhaled the smell she associated with the man who lived here. She found a clean towel in a cabinet behind the door, turned on the shower, and stepped into the white-tiled enclosure. The steaming spray felt good against her skin, and she stood with her back to the shower, wetting down her thick hair. She lathered up with some of Cade's shampoo, noticing it was an economy brand rather than one of the more expensive salon brands she preferred. She backed under the warm spray, closing her eyes and lifting her arms to rinse the lather from her hair. She heard, rather than saw, the shower door open, and felt Cade's body brush against her as he stepped into the shower.

"Morning, beautiful," he said in a sleepy voice. "I thought maybe you could use some help in here."

"Oh you did, did you?" she replied teasingly. "I can always use help from a big, strong cowboy." Sage ran her hands up and down his muscular arms and shoulders, liking how the water cast a sheen over his tanned skin, how it ran in rivulets down his chest flattening his thick, curly chest hair. Picking up the bar of soap, she rubbed it over his torso until a creamy lather formed. Then, while she washed his arms and shoulders, she made sure her breasts rubbed against him. His erection poked against her belly as if asking for attention, and she answered by running the slick bar of soap around his genitals until they were slippery with bubbles.

"I think it's my turn to wash you," Cade whispered, moaning as her hands continued to wash him.

"What's the matter, cowboy?" she teased. "Can't you take it?" His hands caressed her soapy breasts as she continued to fondle his penis. "I think you like this a lot," she said softly, her voice and hands arousing him beyond anything he'd ever felt. "You're so big and hard. I can't believe how long and thick your cock gets when I touch you." Her words drove him over the edge, and he groaned loudly as his semen sprayed her chest and belly. Pulling the bar of soap from her fingers, he washed his sticky, white cum from her, and then returned the favor, rubbing the slippery soap between her thighs. His hot soapy fingers brought her to a quick and intense orgasm. She'd been so aroused by his response to her that it hadn't taken much to bring on her own release.

He left the shower first, and when Sage got out, she combed her hair with the little black comb, used her finger to brush her teeth, slipped on Cade's shirt, and headed to the kitchen where she smelled bacon frying. Cade whistled appreciatively when he saw her in his shirt. His kitchen in the mobile home was tiny, and separated from the living room by a bar. The trailer was an older model, its décor reminiscent of the early eighties. Sage knew that Lloyd had bought it used, although it had been here for a long time, probably at least ten years. Several other hired hands had lived in it before Cade, and it showed the scars. The tan shag carpet was worn thin in spots, and the wood paneling had nail holes where previous residents had hung pictures. Cade's living room was like the bathroom in that nothing decorative had been added; His worn green sofa and an old faux leather chair sat in front of the television, obviously grouped to give the best angle for viewing the screen.

Her inspection was interrupted by the sound of plates being set on the bar, and she turned to see Cade place two plates filled with bacon, scrambled eggs, and toast in front of the bar stools. He turned and picked up two cups of steaming black coffee and sat them beside the plates.

"Do you need sugar?" he questioned. "I don't have any cream so you're out of luck there."

"No, black is fine." She conceded. Sage climbed up onto the nearest bar stool, picked up her fork, and dug in with gusto. Their night of loving had left her famished. Cade chuckled.

"You're hungry too, I see," he said and began eating his own food with the same enthusiasm Sage showed.

"These eggs are wonderful!" she complimented. "What's your secret?"

"No secret, really," he answered. "I get fresh eggs from Roberta Williams. They're a lot better than the store-bought ones. I just whip them up with a little whole milk, some salt and pepper, and scramble them in butter."

"No wonder they're good!" She said with a laugh, "whole milk and butter, not to mention the fresh eggs. They're bound to be delicious." They made small talk during breakfast, and Sage offered to clean up the kitchen since Cade had to get to work. She was up to her elbows in hot sudsy water when a knock at the door startled her. She looked down at her skimpy attire, and hollered at Cade.

"Someone's at the door," she announced. He walked out of the bedroom, tucking his shirt into his jeans as he headed for the entrance. He quickly buttoned up, and then opened the door, smiling as he saw Lloyd through the screen.

"Morning Cade," Lloyd began. "Is Sage here?" he questioned, a note of urgency in his voice. From the kitchen, Sage heard her name, and the sound in Lloyd's voice, and she felt an awful fear rise in her chest.

CHAPTER TEN

"I'm here, Lloyd," Sage called out. "Is something wrong?" She felt a tremor in her voice. She rounded the end of the bar and was at the front door before she could even think about what she was wearing, and how it would look. Lloyd's eyes took in the scene, but Cade saw no judgment in his expression, only concern for Sage.

"Your grandma had a bad spell early this morning, and they took her to the emergency room. She's stable, but they need you to get down there right away." Lloyd explained.

"Just a minute, and I'll be right there," Sage said as she hurried into the bedroom and began throwing her clothes on as fast as she could. In a matter of minutes, she was out the front door.

"I'll take you," Lloyd offered. "My trucks right here ready to go." With a distracted wave in Cade's direction, she climbed into Lloyd's truck, her face masked in worry. Lloyd was right behind her, and they sped away from the sale barn and toward the hospital on the northwest corner of town.

"When the hospital couldn't reach you at home, they called me to see if I knew where you were." Lloyd explained. "Cade mentioned that you two were going for supper, so I took a chance that you'd be at his house. And don't be embarrassed, Sage. You're both grown-ups and I'm not one for gossip."

"Thanks Lloyd," Sage responded, relief in her voice. She'd always had so much respect for Lloyd as her boss and as a friend, that she would have felt really bad if he changed his opinion of her because she spent the night with Cade. In a few minutes, they pulled up to the entrance of the hospital, and Lloyd let her out at the front door, and then went to park his truck. Nina Claremont was a friend of his, and he intended to stay with Sage and see this through. Sage's grandpa, Henry Claremont, had been a valued customer at the sale barn for many years, and a fast friendship had developed between the two men. When Lloyd entered Nina's hospital room, Sage stood by her bed holding the older woman's hand between hers, a look of concern marred her brow.

Sage's first glimpse of her beloved grandma Nina, looking pale and weak on the hospital bed, brought on a rush of guilt. *Had Grandma tried to call her during the night and she hadn't been home?* Sage's mind raced through all the times she had needed her Grandma, and Nina had always been there for her. She couldn't bear the thought that in her Grandma's time of need, she had been unavailable. Tears slid down her cheeks as she held her Grandma's hands. The green bleeps on the heart monitor, the tubes and wires hooked up to Nina's body, and the sterile environment of the hospital seemed to overpower her normally strong grandmother. At the touch of Sage's hand, Nina's eyes opened gradually, and a weak smile touched her lips.

"Sage," she whispered.

"I'm here now Grandma. It'll be okay." Sage comforted her.

"I'm feeling better now, darling," Nina tried to reassure her granddaughter. "The doctor's aren't sure what's wrong. They're going to run some tests." But Sage could tell Nina wasn't feeling better. Her pallor and weakness frightened Sage, but she did her best to hide it.

"I'll talk to the doctors soon, Grandma. They'll tell me what's wrong, and what tests they're going to run." Nina seemed encouraged by Sage's presence, and smiled hopefully.

"Are you Nina's granddaughter?" a low feminine voice asked from the doorway. Sage looked up to see a woman in a white lab coat. *This must be the new doctor*, she thought.

"Yes. I'm Sage Claremont," she responded. The woman walked to Sage with her hand outstretched. Her firm handshake, combined with a warm smile, soon put Sage at ease with the doctor.

"My name is Susan Rommel," she said in a friendly, confident voice, "Nice to meet you Sage."

"Likewise," Sage smiled back.

"I'd like to discuss your grandmother's condition with you and her, if that's okay?"

"Definitely," Sage said eagerly.

"The test results show that Nina had a slight heart attack this morning. Unfortunately, we don't have the facilities here to determine just how much damage was done. I feel it's best that she be transferred to a larger hospital where more tests can be done to see just how serious her problem is, and what can be done about it. If the tests are done in a larger hospital, then should she require any surgery or other procedure it could be done right there," Dr. Rommel explained. Turning to Sage, she continued. "Nina mentioned that her son lives in the Denver area. Would that be your father?" She noted Sage's quick nod. "Would you like me to set up her transfer to a hospital there? That way you would both have family close by. That is, if you plan on going Sage? I guess I'm just assuming that you will."

"Of course I'm going," Sage said adamantly.

"I'll get the transport set up and arrange for hospital accommodations. She'll be going on an air ambulance. I feel the drive in a regular ambulance would be too much for her. You can ride in the helicopter too, Sage. They allow one family member to go on the flight. The chopper should arrive here in about an hour, so you have a little time to get your things together. Can you be at the airport by 10:00 a.m.?"

"I'll be there." Sage answered.

"Pack lightly," Dr. Rommel directed. "There isn't much extra room on the helicopter."

After the doctor left, Sage and Lloyd reassured Nina that she would be fine, and they left so Sage could get her things. Lloyd waited while she packed, and then took her to the little airport so she wouldn't have to leave her car setting out the whole time she was gone.

"Lloyd, can you see that my garden gets watered while I'm gone?" She asked on the drive to the plane. "I have some plants in the house also. Two are in the kitchen and one in the living room. They only need watered about once a week, but they're due for a drink today. Hopefully, I'll be back home before they need watered again."

"Sure thing, Sage," he agreed. "I'll take care of everything. Don't you worry."

Sage thought to herself that it was a good thing there was no sale this week. Not having to worry about the café until next week took a load off of her mind.

"Oh, and Lloyd?" she began. "Please tell Cade what happened, and that I'll call him as soon as I know anything."

"I'll tell him," the older man assured her. Sage grabbed her small suitcase and slammed the pickup door. The helicopter was just landing on a helipad near the small terminal, and the ambulance, with Grandma Nina inside, was waiting near the tarmac. They boarded the air ambulance, and Sage was seated in a rear-facing seat behind the cockpit. She could see Nina on the stretcher, and as soon as they took off, her grandma seemed to fall asleep. Sage leaned her head back against the seat and gazed out the window at the open prairie land with its wide, rolling hills. Dark green, tree-lined creeks meandered along shallow valleys beneath the plane.

While she was at home, she'd taken time to call her parents and let them know what was going on. Of course, they was very concerned, and promised they'd meet the helicopter at the hospital. She'd be so glad to see both of them, so glad to have someone to share the responsibility of decision-making and someone to help shoulder the worry.

CHAPTER ELEVEN

Sage stepped off the helicopter and onto the roof of St. Christopher's Hospital in Denver. She looked out across the city skyline at the Rocky Mountains. Their awesome beauty never failed to amaze her, though this time her appreciation was short-lived as she stepped aside for the medics to pull Grandma Nina's stretcher out and onto the helipad. Sage took her grandma's hand and walked beside the stretcher. Nina smiled wanly as she was wheeled across the roof and through double doors, then into an elevator near the entrance. The group emerged near the main desk of the cardiac unit, and Sage saw her father sitting in a nearby lounge. She kissed her grandma and gave what she hoped was an encouraging smile, before the older woman was whisked into an examination room. Sage turned and moved toward her father, who was reading the *Rocky Mountain News*, unaware that the flight from Kansas had arrived.

"Dad?" Sage's voice cracked as she walked into the visitor's lounge. Her father stood up, and she rushed into his arms as tears poured down her cheeks.

"Hey, baby," he whispered as he pulled her close. She breathed in his familiar and comforting scent as her tears dampened the shoulder of his flannel shirt. "It's okay. The doctors will figure out what grandma needs, and she'll be back home soon. I'm sure of it." The note of confidence in his voice sounded forced, but Sage appreciated the effort. She knew it was childish, but all she wanted was for someone to tell her everything would be okay.

Sage lowered herself onto the sofa while her dad filled a Styrofoam cup with strong, black coffee and brought it to her.

"Thanks," she accepted the cup gratefully. "It's been a stressful morning, to say the least." Sage filled her Dad in on the morning's happenings, *well, the pertinent ones at least*, she thought, as she sipped the hot liquid. They sat talking for nearly an hour until Don Claremont declared his stomach was rumbling, and went to check with a nurse and find out how much longer the wait might be.

He returned to his daughter, a pager in hand, "The nurse says we may as well go to the cafeteria and get something to eat. She'll page us if we're needed." Relieved to have something to take her mind off her worries, Sage followed her father to the elevator, then down a series of corridors as they followed the signs toward the huge hospital's food court.

After polishing off slightly dry ham sandwiches, barbecue chips and diet sodas, the pair returned to the cardiac waiting room. It wasn't long until the doctor emerged, an attractive, gray-haired woman who appeared to be in her late fifties. Her kind smile and professional demeanor was instantly comforting to Sage.

"Hi, my name is Dr. Werner," she began, extending a hand to Don first and then to Sage. "I'm a cardiologist, and I'm the one who examined Nina. Your mother had a minor heart-attack this morning, Mr. Claremont," she explained. "There wasn't a lot of damage, but she has two blockages that need to be opened. One is seventy percent closed, and the other eighty-five. We can put in stents right away."

"What kind of recovery are we looking at here?" Don queried. "Will she be back to her old self?"

"Pretty much," Dr. Werner explained. "She seems to be in good shape for her age, and even though it will take her longer to get her strength back than it would a younger patient, she should make a full recovery."

"What time frame are we looking at?" Don asked.

"She should be back to her regular routine in two to three months," replied Dr. Werner. Sage breathed a sigh of relief.

"See? What did I tell you?" Don smiled at Sage. Then looking back to Dr. Werner he continued. "How long will she be in the hospital after the surgery?"

"We usually keep patients three to five days, depending on how well they are doing. Then I'd like to have her close by for another month so she can come in for weekly checkups. Will that be a problem, Mr. Claremont?" Dr. Werner glanced down at Nina's chart. "I see you live here in Denver."

"I do," Don confirmed. "That won't be a problem at all."

"Can we see Grandma Nina now?" Sage spoke up.

"You sure can," Dr. Werner smiled. "Follow me." She turned and led Sage and Don a short way down the brightly lit corridor and into a circular room where five patients were on beds separated by white curtains suspended from tracks in the ceiling.

Nina managed a smile when Don and Sage walked in.

"Sounds like I'm going to have that balloon surgery," she announced.

"How are you feeling, Grandma?" Sage queried. "You look better than you did earlier. You sure had us worried this morning."

"I had myself worried this morning," Nina admitted. "Thought for a little while I was a goner the way my chest felt."

"We're glad you're all right mom," Don comforted her. "The doctor said she can get you fixed right up. You'll be back to your usual in a couple months."

"Sounds like it," Nina replied. "I'll sure be glad to get this over with. Doesn't sound like much fun having something threaded through my veins that way. But Doctor Werner said I wouldn't feel a thing, so I told her it was okay." Nina was obviously pleased with her decision to go ahead with the procedure. Sage smiled.

"There's the feisty woman I know and love," she teased.

Sage and her father left the hospital a while later to get a snack. They found a mom and pop grill near the hospital, and Sage ordered a huge salad topped with chicken bits and crispy tortilla strips. She was starving! Her breakfast with Cade seemed like two days ago instead of that morning, and the she'd left half of the dry sandwich from the hospital cafeteria on her plate. Don placed his order, and they both sat back with a sigh of relief and let themselves relax.

"I'll need to find somewhere to buy some clothes." Sage tried to think of what she would need. "I wasn't allowed to bring much on the helicopter this morning, plus when I knew Grandma and the ambulance were at the airport ready for the flight, I just wanted to get there as fast as possible."

"There's a shopping center on the way home where you should be able to get anything you'd need." Don suggested. "We'll swing by there after the procedure."

"I at least want to stay here till Grandma gets out of the hospital," Sage told her dad. "But I can't stay for a month. Lloyd has a special horse sale coming up that will be a big job for me. And that's on top of the regular livestock sales I have to cook for, plus the book I'm working on needs my attention."

"How's your writing coming along?" he queried. "I haven't heard you say much about it when we've talked on the phone."

"My book is coming along great. I'm really excited about it," Sage's eyes sparkled with animation. "I also have an article submitted to several writing magazines about the creative process. I really hope it sells because it'd be nice to have that extra income while I'm finishing the book. Who knows how long it might take to get it submitted, and then I don't know if anyone will publish it." Sage's voice trailed off.

Their food arrived, and they dug in with gusto. Four o'clock in the afternoon was late for lunch. And for Sage, it was really five o'clock since her body was used to central time. They ate in companionable silence. Sage and her Dad both declined dessert, but drank a cup of coffee to ward off the tiredness that was overtaking them. They left the restaurant and drove back to the hospital to be with Nina. After the surgery was over, Don stayed with his mother, and Sage drove to a shopping center to get herself outfitted with enough clothes and toiletries for the next week.

That night, lying in her bed in the room she'd had growing up, Sage dialed Cade's number. As the phone rang, she imagined his sweet voice melting over her. "Hello, beautiful," she pictured him saying, but the ringing continued. She hung up after the tenth ring. He didn't have an answering machine. As she drifted off, sleepy images of where he might be floated through her mind; he's probably helping Lloyd get in some cattle, she told herself right before the warm, darkness of sleep washed over her.

CHAPTER TWELVE

Sage and her mom made their way back to the hospital in the inky, pre-dawn coolness. Renee Claremont's arm was around her daughter's shoulders when they stepped off the elevator and onto the cardiac wing. She gave Sage a squeeze, then followed her daughter into Nina's room. They found Don sleeping in a chair next to his mother's bed.

"Good morning," Sage announced their arrival as Nina looked over with a smile. "How was your night?" She continued.

"Just like you'd expect." She described the numerous times she'd been awakened to have her blood pressure and temperature taken. "Nonetheless," she went on, her voice threaded with a feisty undertone, "I'm glad the surgery is over with, and I'll be glad to get home."

"You'll be out of here before you know it," Renee encouraged her mother-in-law. "I bet you'll be surprised at how much better you feel once you're recovered. As much blockage as you had, it had to be making your heart work a lot harder. You might be amazed at how much more energy you have."

"I hope you're right," Nina's weak smile betrayed her worry.

"I'm sure she is, Grandma," Sage added. "I bet by next summer you'll have the whole garden whipped into shape!"

"The garden looks wonderful already, and you know it," Nina smiled.

"Thanks to all your help," Sage leaned over and hugged Nina just as Doctor Werner entered the curtained area.

"Good morning, Mrs. Claremont?" Her confident smile encompassed the group. " You're a lucky woman." She continued. "Other than the heart blockages, you're in pretty good shape. With the stents in place, you should make a strong recovery."

"All your exercise is paying off, Grandma," Sage interjected. "Gardening is good for you."

Dr. Werner reviewed Nina's chart. "Do you have any questions before I go?"

"I've asked all the questions I can think of," the older woman's independence was a breath of fresh air. "Take good care of me doc. My granddaughter and I have a big garden to take care of."

"Only the best care, Mrs. Claremont," Dr. Werner smiled as she turned and left. Immediately, a nurse came in and began checking Nina's vitals.

"Time to get ready for breakfast, Mrs. Claremont," the young nurse announced just as a man in scrubs walked in with the breakfast tray. The nurse recorded the blood pressure, pulse and temperature reading.

"See you an about an hour, Mrs. Claremont." She smiled as left the room.

"We'll be right back, Mom," Don reassured her. "We're going to the cafeteria for coffee. Love you."

"I love you too, honey," Nina said, her voice sounded sleepy. Sage watched her grandma's eyes close, then turned and walked toward the family waiting area.

*   *   *   *   *   *   *

On the pretense of using the restroom, Sage went out to the main lobby and punched in Cade's number on her cell phone. *Surely he's home at this hour*, she told herself. She held her breath in anticipation for the first couple of rings, and then exhaled dejectedly when she realized he wasn't home. She really needed to hear his voice. Determined not to be upset, she marched into the hospital cafeteria, spied her parents sitting at a corner table with three steaming cups of coffee, and headed toward them. They decided to take their coffees back to Nina's room to be with her while she ate.

*   *   *   *   *   *   *

They sat with Nina, drinking their coffee while she spooned oatmeal into her mouth, complaining between bites about its blandness.

"Couldn't they put a little salt and butter in this?" She grumbled.

As they talked, Sage noticed that her father's voice had lost some of the tension she had picked up on earlier. She was so upset about her Grandmother's illness, and she couldn't imagine how scary it must be for her Dad. Just thinking about her own mother having any health problems was terrifying to Sage. Her Grandma being sick was bad enough.

"Let's get out of here," Don whispered when Nina had finished eating and dozed off.

"I need another cup of coffee and something in my belly."

"I'm with you," Renee grabbed her husband's hand. "Come on, honey," she directed Sage, and the three of them headed for the elevator.

*   *   *   *   *   *   *   *

The week had passed quickly, Sage reflected as she stared out the window of her parent's kitchen. The big back yard's lush greenness undulated in the crisp mountain air. At this elevation, as soon as the sun dropped behind the Rockies, the air cooled quickly. Sage could remember lying on her back in the soft grass, staring at the sky and waiting for the first star to appear so she could make a wish. Grandma Nina was recovering here. She'd gotten released from the hospital yesterday, and was already getting back to her feisty self, although she still tired easily. It had been so nice last night to see Grandma's blue eyes sparkling at her from across the table, teasing her about Cade.

"So how's that boyfriend of yours?" She asked with a mischievous wink.

"Boyfriend?" Don jumped into the conversation. "I hadn't heard about any boyfriend."

"Me either," Renee smiled. "Would you like to tell us about him?" She looked at Sage.

"He's a real looker," Nina piped up. "Tall, dark and handsome; a cowboy too."

"Mom," Renee reproached her teasingly, "I want Sage to tell us about him."

Sage blushed furiously. *Oh well*, she thought, *this was bound to happen.* She was surprised Grandma Nina hadn't mentioned Cade to her parents on the phone. "His name is Cade Lofton, and he works for Lloyd at the sale barn. He's been there about three months I guess."

"How long have you been seeing him," Renee queried?

"A few weeks now," Sage explained. "He's a nice guy, a real gentleman," she went on," but I don't know a whole lot about his background. I know he's a hard worker and Lloyd has a lot of respect for him that way," her voice trailed off.

"Well," Don began," there's a lot to be said for someone who works hard. In this day and age, that isn't a given."

"That's for sure," Grandma Nina piped up, "And besides that, those sweet brown eyes of his give me a toothache!" Sage blushed again.

"Okay, enough picking on Sage." Renee stood up. "Don, could you help me clear the table so Sage can go visit with her Grandma. Since she's heading home soon, they won't get a chance for a face-to-face chat for a few weeks." With a big sigh, Don rose from his chair and began to pick up dirty dishes. "You're worse than the kids were when they were little," Renee laughed, giving him a pat on the backside.

*   *   *   *   *   *   *   *

"Sage, honey," Nina spoke softly, "I hope you know I was only teasing you in there. I think Cade is a wonderful guy, and I can tell how much you like him."

"I can take teasing, grandma, you know that." The sparkle in Sage's eyes made Nina smile.

"How is Cade doing, by the way?" Nina inquired. "I presume you've spoken with him since we've been here?"

"Actually," Sage confessed. "I haven't been able to reach him. I've tried a couple of times and he hasn't been home. He doesn't have an answering machine or cell phone or anything like that."

"Oh honey," Nina slipped an arm around Sage's shoulder as they sat next to each other on the sofa. "I'm sure he's busy with sale barn work. You've just called at the wrong times.

"I'm sure your right, Grandma. I think I'll go try him again right now." Sage smiled at her grandma as she scooped the cordless phone up from the end table and carried it to her room.

    *   *   *   *   *

"Hello?" The sound of Cade's deep voice melted her like whipped cream over hot fudge sauce. Lying across her bed in the dark room, Sage smiled.

"Hey, cowboy, I've been missing you."

"You have?" He teased. "Which part of me have you been missing?"

Sage blushed. "All of you," she replied, "but some parts in particular."

She smiled again at Cade's chuckle.

"Has Lloyd been keeping you busy?"

"And then some," he began. "We got in a shipment of cattle from North Dakota; yearlings to run on grass until they're ready for the feed yard this fall. I've been doing a lot of doctoring. A few of them are escape artists, so I chase after them too."

"I thought you must be swamped," Sage sympathized. "I've tried calling a few times and couldn't get you."

"How's your grandma?" Cade queried.

"She's doing great!" Sage voiced the encouragement they all felt. "She came home from the hospital yesterday. She had to have some stents put in, but her heart wasn't damaged too badly from the attack. She's supposed to stay here for a month so she can have check-ups." Sage continued, "I suppose I'll be coming home soon, whenever Dad has time to bring me. I can't wait to see you." He could hear the smile in her voice.

"Same here," he said quietly. "I may be taking off for a few days as soon as these cattle get settled in."

"Oh yeah?" Sage struggled to keep the disappointment out of her voice. "Where you gonna go?"

"There's something I need to see about, back in the place I used to live." His vague answer made Sage uncomfortable, but she tried not to let him know.

"I hope I get to see you before you take off." She kept her tone light.

"Yeah, we'll see." Cade replied. "Guess it depends on when you get here."

"Guess so," she answered. "I better go now. It's been a long day." Sage couldn't keep the worry out of her voice. "I'll call you when I know what day I'm coming home."

"Okay," Cade could hear the worry in her voice, and he felt himself closing down. He wasn't ready to tell her what was going on. "Give me your number there." Cade asked, jotting it down as she recited it. "I'll be talking to you, babe," he finished.

"Bye," Sage said softly before hanging up. She lay there, not knowing whether to be happy she'd reached him, or worried about what he'd said. Not wanting to face her grandma's questions about the phone call, Sage changed into her pajamas and crawled into her bed. Despite her unsettling thoughts, she fell asleep quickly.

*   *   *   *   *

Cade lay back on his sofa, his thoughts on Sage's phone call. He knew she'd been upset when he told her he had to take off for a few days. He felt bad, but pulled inside himself, like he always did when it came to talking about his childhood. He knew if she found out the whole truth about where he came from, she run the other way. He couldn't bring himself to face that. He turned on his side and stared at the Matlock re-run, not really listening.

He'd gotten a phone call the day after Sage's departure. It had been a lawyer from Canyon Ridge, the town where he'd finished high school.

"Is this Cade Lofton?" The woman's friendly voice didn't stop him from tensing up. "The Cade Lofton who worked for Sam Tyler about thirteen years ago?"

"Yeah, this is him."

"Wow! I've been looking for you for a long time, Mr. Lofton." Relief threaded the woman's voice. "I'm Ruth Jamison, the lawyer overseeing Mr. Tyler's estate." Cade sunk into a chair.

"Sam's dead?" He uttered. "When?"

"Actually, Mr. Tyler died about eighteen months ago," the lawyer explained. "I've been trying to find you ever since then."

"What happened to him?" Cade wanted to know. "What about Carol? Is she okay?" Cade remembered Sam's wife, the woman who had cared about him and treated him with decency and respect when he'd needed it the most.

"Mrs. Tyler died of breast cancer about nine years ago. Sam had a heart attack." Ruth Jamison heard Cade's sharp intake of breath. "I'm sorry," she continued. "I thought you knew."

"I didn't," Cade's voice was tight. "I haven't been in touch with them since I left," he admitted.

"Well, as you know the Tyler's didn't have any children," Ms. Jamison continued. "Mr. Tyler named you as a beneficiary in his will. I'd like to you meet with me here in Canyon Ridge to go over the details. When could you be here?" She finished.

A beneficiary? Sam was dead? and Carol too? And they'd left him something? Cade was reeling from shock at all the information he'd been given.

"Mr. Lofton? Are you okay?" Ruth Jamison's voice brought him back to the present.

"Yeah," Cade mumbled. "It's just a lot to take in all at once. The Tyler's meant a lot to me."

"Apparently you meant a lot to them too." Her voice reassured Cade.

"Is it possible for you to be here in the near future?" She again queried.

"I think so," Cade's thoughts were a jumble. All he could think about were that Sam and Carol were gone, and he'd never gotten in touch with them; never told them how much they'd meant to him. "I'll talk to my boss today and see when I can take off."

"That'd be great!" She gave him the number at her office, then said goodbye.

Cade sat on his sofa in a daze, his mind drifting back to the time he'd spent at the Tyler ranch in Canyon Ridge, Nebraska. He remembered the rough terrain of the canyons, and the flat, top land where irrigated corn grew in lush rows beneath center pivot sprinklers. He remembered the Tyler's home place; its well-kept appearance; the cozy ranch house whose wrap-around porch overlooked the narrow valley's lush, alfalfa greenness. The smell of fresh coffee and bacon frying still took him back to those early summer mornings when he'd arrived at their place for work, stuck his head in the back door, and heard Carol's voice call out, "Get yourself in here, young man. Your breakfast is gettin' cold!" Those were some of the only times he'd really felt at home since his Dad had died. The Tyler's were the only people who had really cared about him. And now they were gone. And he had never told them how he felt. Tears ran unchecked down his tanned cheeks.

He didn't know how long he'd been sitting there, but a knock on the door pulled him from his memories. Lloyd stuck his head in.

"You ready to go?" He asked.

Turning away quickly to hide his face, Cade mumbled, "Yeah, I'm ready. I'll be right out."

"Bring the other rig, and I'll meet you at the Stinson place. I have the horses in my trailer." Lloyd shut the door and walked toward the white Ford pickup.

The next morning, Cade was headed for Canyon Ridge.

CHAPTER THIRTEEN

Two days later, Sage and her father drove in comfortable silence across the flat, farm country of extreme Western Kansas. The ripening wheat fields rolled in waves of green and gold across huge expanses of fertile land. Sage stared unseeing, lost in her thoughts. She'd called Cade's number twice the day before wanting to tell him when she'd be arriving home. Both times the rings had gone unanswered.

"So sweetie," Don began. "How's the book coming along?"

Her parents had always been so supportive of her writing. She was lucky. Never once had they suggested that she should pursue a different career path, or that she should major in something that would bring her a steady income, because they knew that wasn't her dream.

"It's coming," she turned to him. "My goal has been to write a chapter a week, and so far I've pretty much accomplished that." She chuckled, "But those chapters are only rough drafts; they still need a lot of work!"

Don glanced over with a smile. "Well, just getting the words down on paper is a big step. The fine-tuning is what you like best, if I remember right?" he queried.

"You do remember right, Dad." Sage grinned. "Remember how I spent holiday breaks agonizing over my college papers? How I'd re-write words and sentences and paragraphs over and over again until I thought they were just right? And it drove you so crazy!"

"I remember that all right!" Don laughed. "I never could understand how all that mattered."

"I guess it's a writer's thing," Don's laugh was contagious and Sage couldn't stop herself from giggling when she thought back to how annoyed her Dad would get with her pickiness about her writing. "It all means the same thing. Just put something down and be done with it!" His exasperated voice would rumble through the house.

About an hour from Hope, they drove through a fast food outlet for a sub sandwich, and then ate as they continued their trip. Sage breathed a sigh of relief when they pulled up in front of her little house. She climbed out of the white suburban, retrieved the duffle bag containing the clothes she had purchased in Denver from the backseat, and led the way to her front door.

Don followed her, carrying his own overnight bag. He planned to spend the night at his daughter's, then go to Nina's apartment tomorrow to see what needed to be taken care of. She'd given him a detailed list of the things she'd require for her extended stay in Denver. *Women,* he thought, they *can't go anywhere without taking a whole carload of stuff!*

"I better go over to the sale barn and make sure everything is ready in the café. I lucked out that there was no sale last week," Sage noted. "At least I have all day tomorrow to get ready for this one!"

"I'm going to rest a bit," Don announced. "Then I'll head over to Mom's place and get some arrangements made."

"Okay," Sage tossed her bag on to the floor in her bedroom, and then headed for the door. "I'll plan on having something ready for dinner at 6:30."

*   *   *   *
*

Cade jerked awake, his mind confused by the unusual sounds that had pulled him from sleep. Then he remembered he was in Canyon Ridge, in a motel along the main drag. He wasn't used to hearing traffic noise. His mobile home by the sale barn was on a quiet road at the edge of Hope. Not that Canyon Ridge was metro, not by any stretch of the imagination, but it was bigger than Hope. The four-lane street in front of his motel roared with traffic as people hurried to their jobs.

Stretching his nakedness under the soft, cotton sheets, Cade went over his plan for the day. His meeting with the lawyer, Ruth Jamison, was scheduled for ten. Glancing at his watch, he saw that it was 7:30 now. He didn't usually sleep this late, but he guessed the long drive yesterday, and the emotional trauma of learning about Sam's and Carol's deaths, had just wiped him out. He could easily drift back to sleep, but he knew should probably get up, shower and find a place for some breakfast. He thought of bacon and eggs as sleep overtook him.

At nine forty-five, Cade walked into the Jamison Law Firm. He hoped his newest jeans and light blue western dress shirt were fancy enough for this meeting. They were the best clothes he owned. Being a cowboy, there wasn't much call for dressing up. He didn't even own a suit. He introduced himself to the receptionist; a young woman who Cade didn't think looked old enough to be sitting behind a big desk like that. *She ought to still be in high school!,* he thought.

"Are you Mr. Lofton?" She smiled up at him, "Mrs. Jamison will be with you in a few minutes. May I get you a cup of coffee?"

"Yeah," Cade accepted. "Coffee would be great." She gestured to a sofa in the waiting area. "If you want to have a seat over there, I'll bring you your coffee." He watched her leave the room, his eyes taking in her slender figure. *She's cute,* he thought, *but nowhere near as hot as Sage.* He wondered if Sage was back in Hope yet. He sure had missed her. *Guess I should have called her before I left,* he chided himself. He fished his wallet out of his snug jeans pocket and dug through it. Damn! He'd forgotten the paper with her cell number on it. He meant to grab it off the bar when he left. Later, he'd give her a call at home. Hopefully she was there.

The receptionist came back and handed him a Styrofoam cup of steaming black coffee. He took a sip, then sat back and picked up a copy of the Prairie Journal, flipped it open to the "horses for sale" ads, and began reading. He was focused on a promising ad for a roping horse, a six-year-old gelding with great bloodlines, when the door to his left opened. A tall, thin woman of about forty-five walked out.

"Cade Lofton?" She stuck her hand out. When he nodded, she continued. "I'm Ruth Jamison. I'm glad you were able to make it here so quickly." After handing a few papers to her assistant, Ms. Jamison smiled back at Cade.

"If you'll follow me, we can get started." They walked into her office, a room that was simple, yet warm and comfortable. It fit her, Cade decided. Nice; Classy, yet not pretentious. He hated pretension. Ruth sat down behind her desk, and gestured for him to take a seat in the brown leather chair opposite her. Her gaze was warm and intelligent, her smile friendly; Cade felt himself relaxing a bit. He still couldn't really imagine why he was here.

"You must be very curious about why I asked you to come here." Ruth began.

"I am Ms. Jamison," Cade admitted.

"Please, call me Ruth." She directed. "And may I call you Cade?"

"Sure," Cade smiled. "So, Ruth, I'm very curious. What do you need to tell me?"

"Well, as I mentioned, it's to do with the last will and testament of Sam Tyler." She picked up a thin packet of papers from her desk. "This is Sam's will, written about five years before he died, but after Carol had passed away. You're familiar with the Tyler's ranch?" she queried.

"Yes," Cade reacted by leaning forward in his chair and reaching for his coffee. "I worked for the Tyler's after school and during the summer for a couple of years while I was in high school. They were really good to me, like the parents I didn't have." His voice trailed off.

"You were like a son to them," Ruth explained. "Sam talked about you a lot while I was helping him revise his will. Initially, of course, he was going to leave everything to Carol. But when she preceded him in death, he had no other family. He told me about how much they'd come to care for you, how rough they figured your life must have been. Although, he said you would never talk about it." Cade shifted uncomfortably in his seat. "Anyway," Ruth continued. "Sam saw potential in you. He saw a young man with a good work ethic, good values, someone he knew could achieve a lot if given the chance. Sam wanted to give you that chance."

"Meaning what exactly?" Cade's voice sounded hollow.

"Sam left you his ranch." Ruth made the announcement with a steady voice, watching for his reaction. Cade didn't respond. He was stunned.

"It encompasses about 2,200 acres," she described, "The house and outbuildings, the equipment, and some money in the bank from the sale of his cow herd. He wanted you to have some capital to get started."

"The ranch?" Cade's voice was barely a whisper. "He left me the ranch?"

"That's right, Cade. He left you the ranch." Ruth was smiling now.

"Why would he leave me the ranch? I hadn't seen them in ten years or more. I hadn't even kept in touch!" His tone was disbelieving.

"I know," Ruth sympathized. "Sam told me you thought you had to prove something, to make it on your own. Was he right?"

"I am making it on my own!" Cade was adamant. "I get along just fine."

"Sam knew you would. Still, he wanted to do this. He said you were the only person he knew who would love the place like he had. Was he wrong?" Ruth asked softly.

"No," Cade took a deep breath. "I always dreamed of having a place like that. It's what I was working toward." He confessed. "With my pay, it was a ways off, but I would have done it!"

"I'm sure you would have," Ruth agreed. "You'll have your work cut out for you anyway. The place has been empty since Sam died. A neighbor, Cliff Barnes, has been putting up the hay. I hired him to do it."

"I don't know what to say," Cade's voice was still tinged with disbelief. "I just can't believe it."

"How about we drive out and take a look at the place?" Ruth offered.

Cade stood up. "Good idea!" His grin was infectious.

CHAPTER FOURTEEN

Cade climbed into the black SUV next to Ruth Jamison. He inhaled the scent of new leather and his eyes took in the expensive features on the faux-wood dash. Classical music wafted from speakers all around him when Ruth cranked the engine up. She quickly turned the air conditioner on high. The day was promising to be a scorcher. Cade watched for familiar landmarks as they drove to the edge of town. He saw some stores he recognized, and they drove past the street where his foster parents had lived, but their house had been six or eight blocks down; too far away to see; not that he wanted to see it anyway.

"Remember the corner," Ruth queried as she slowed to turn north?

"I remember." Cade felt a lump in his throat when they turned on the gravel road. The old windmill that had stood in the corner of the pasture to his right had been replaced with a newer version, but he would always remember how to get to Sam's place. The route was burned into his mind; the eagerness he felt as he drove to the ranch, and the dread he experienced when he headed back to the foster home.

Ahead he could see a large, red barn next to a tall silo.

"Who lives there now," he asked, nodding his head toward the farm? "It used to be the Young's didn't it?"

"Yes," Ruth smiled. "And it's still the Young's," she continued, but the youngest son, Pete, and his wife run the place now. When you were here Harlan Young was farming. He and Eleanor live in town now, and spend the winters in Arizona." She laughed, "Harlan still spends plenty of time at the farm though, every chance he gets."

"Harlan's a good guy," Cade reminisced. "Sam and I used to help him with his cattle sometimes. I remember the brandings! Eleanor put on a feast for all of us. I haven't had a meal like that in years." His voice trailed off as he thought of the long table set up in the yard under huge cottonwoods. "She grilled steaks as big as a plate," he chuckled. "You had to eat part of your steak before you could take any other food!"

"I can imagine," Ruth grinned. "Eleanor's quite a woman." They rode on in silence. Cade found the music relaxing. He watched the familiar road unroll before him. The Tyler ranch was twelve miles from town along a winding, hilly road. Part of the route followed the Sappa Creek. In this part of the country, you could tell where the water was. Trees snaked along the valley following the curves and bows of the waterway. The hills were covered with waving prairie grass, but only an occasional tree. Fence lines of barbed wire tautly stretched between wood posts coated in creosote ran along the roadside ditches, occasionally cutting across the open pastures.

Cattle dotted the hillsides grazing on the thick grass, or chewing their cud under the lazy, summer sun.

The miles slipped away, and Cade's anticipation grew when he saw the mailbox atop a wagon wheel. He remembered Sam buying that wagon wheel at a farm auction and how Carol decided it should lean against the mailbox post for decoration. He'd always liked the way it looked there, and the fact that he'd helped with the placement. It made him feel like he was part of their family.

"I helped Sam put that wagon wheel by the mailbox," Cade told Ruth. "We'd gone to an auction that day, and Sam bought the wheel for little of nothing. It was in good shape too." Cade's eyes sparkled. "He was excited 'cause he got such a great deal. He was always looking for antiques. Carol used to tease him about the 'junk' he brought home, but I think she liked it too."

The pulled up in front of the house as he finished his story.

"Here we are," Ruth announced.

Cade's eyes took in the place. His memories had turned it into a fairy-tale setting, but it sure wasn't that now. The yard was overgrown and the house looked dark and empty.

"I've checked inside the house every few months," Ruth explained. "Everything's fine, it just needs a good cleaning." They walked onto the wide wrap-around porch, and she grabbed the door knob and jiggled the key into the lock. "I didn't try to keep up the yard. It wasn't much anyway." She continued. "I know when Carol was alive it looked like something from Home and Garden, but after she died Sam pretty much let it go. He mowed the grass, but that was about it."

Ruth pushed the back door open and stepped aside, letting Cade lead the way into the ranch house kitchen. It was pretty much how Cade remembered it. Pine cabinets topped with blue Formica lined two walls, and an island of the same materials stood in the center of the room. The built in stove looked different, Cade thought, but the deep, white sink was still there. He and Carol had some good talks standing there washing dishes. For a second, he could hear her laughing as she flicked him with bubbles. When he sighed, reality intruded. The air smelled of dust and staleness. He could hear Ruth walking around the living room.

"It's like I remember," he said, mostly to himself.

"What?" Ruth asked brightly, as she stuck her head in the kitchen.

"It's like I remember." He repeated, looking around, trying to take in every detail. "The furniture's still here," he noticed. "I wasn't sure what to expect." He glanced at Ruth as she stood beside him.

"Yes," she described. "He left you the whole shebang; furniture and all. I cleaned out the fridge and freezer, got rid of the perishables and when I couldn't reach you right away, I gave the non-perishable things to the food pantry in town."

"That's good," Cade's throat had a lump again. *I should have been here to do those things,* he chastised himself. *I should have kept in touch and been here.*

"Well," Ruth walked toward the door. "I see Cliff pulling in. I want to ask him about the hay. I'll leave you to look around."

Cade heard the screen door slam behind Ruth as he walked into the living room. This room was the biggest one in the house, with a huge stone fireplace on the north side. The house was L-shaped, with the kitchen and living room on one side, and three bedrooms and a bath in the other wing. Cade checked them all. He couldn't fathom that this was all his. He expected Sam or Carol to walk in at any minute. He looked in the closet in their room, and was relieved to see their clothes were gone. He supposed Ruth had taken care of that too.

After checking out the house, Cade headed for the barn. Sam's old Chevy pickup was parked inside, along with an old baler and some moldy hay. All in all, the structure was sound, he decided. There were also an old granary, and a chicken coop. Carol always kept a few hens for fresh eggs. Maybe he'd get some of his own, he thought. Turning, he saw Ruth walking toward him. Cliff was driving toward the lower hay field on a new-looking John Deere tractor, round-baler in tow. Cade had noticed the purple blooms on the hay when they drove in, a sign that it was time to swath.

"What do you think?" Ruth looked around as she approached. "It's in pretty good shape, huh?"

"Great shape!" Cade watched her. "I still can't believe this is mine now."

"I'm sure it seems strange," Ruth empathized. "I'm just glad I finally found you, and that you know it's yours," she laughed.

"You're not the only one who's glad!" Cade's retort brought on another chuckle. "So, what's next?"

"Well, if you're done looking around here," Ruth began. "We can head back to town, grab some lunch, and get the paperwork taken care of."

"Sounds like a plan," Cade agreed. "I just noticed how hungry I am. Is the dairy king still in business?"

"You're in luck," she said.

"I used to think their onion rings were the best thing ever!" He laughed again. *I haven't laughed this much for a long time,* Cade thought to himself. *I probably sound like a kid on Christmas morning.*

"I feel like a kid on Christmas morning," he confessed to Ruth as they drove back to town.

"In your shoes, so would I," she vowed.

*　　　　*　　　　*　　　　*　　　　*

Sage stepped into the stuffy, heat of the sale barn café. Lloyd didn't run the air conditioner in here except on sale days, which was understandable, Sage knew, but it was hot enough to fry an egg after having been closed up for two weeks. She propped the doors open and turned on the fans, then took stock. Thank God she'd vacuumed and cleaned up after the last sale so she didn't have that mess to face.

When she was taking stock of her supplies, she heard the door to the office slam, and poked her head out of the kitchen to see who was there. Lloyd's bald pate was bent over his desk, his hand punching numbers on the calculator. Sage opened the door between the café and the office.

"Hey Lloyd, I'm back!" she announced.

"I guess you are," he grinned, standing up. "How's your grandma doing?"

"She's on the mend," Sage explained. "Things could have been a lot worse."

"They sure could have," Lloyd agreed. "Glad you're back," he continued. "Did your Dad bring you?"

"Yeah," Sage informed him. "He's over at Grandma's place taking care of stuff. He has to pack a suitcase for her. She sent him a big list of what to get!"

"I'm sure she did," Lloyd chuckled. "Nina always knows just what she wants."

"Is Cade around?" Sage finally got a chance to ask. "He told me he might be gone for a few days."

"He is gone," Lloyd told her. "Didn't say where he was going; only that he'd be back in time for the sale day after tomorrow."

"Okay," Sage sighed. "He didn't tell me where he was going either. I thought it seemed kinda weird, but I guess it's his life."

"I'm sure he'll tell you when he gets back," Lloyd reassured her.

"Yes," Sage forced a smile. "I'm sure he will."

She headed back to the café, made a grocery list, planned a noon special, and then drove to the grocery store. Her fridge at home was bare too. Well, not really bare, but most of the food she'd left would have to be thrown out. Her hasty departure had prevented any opportunity for cleaning out the fridge. Walking into the cool supermarket, she grabbed a cart and headed down aisle one.

*　　　　*　　　　*　　　　*　　　　*

For dinner, Sage made a crisp salad of mixed greens picked fresh from her garden. She fried thick hamburgers, and topped them with sliced tomatoes and sweet onion, then opened a bag of salty, vinegar potato chips and set it on the table. Don walked in as she was taking the burgers from the skillet.

"Hey sweetie," he announced his arrival. "Smells wonderful in here; and boy am I starving!"

Sage laughed. "Did you get Grandma's list filled?" Amusement tinged her voice. "I bet the suburban's full."

"It is," Don groaned. "I just don't know about you women folk."

"Supper's ready," she stated, and sat down at the table.

*　　　　*　　　　*　　　　*

Lying in bed that evening, Sage tried to focus on the magazine article she was reading. Her mind kept returning to Cade, to where he was and why he hadn't told anyone where he was going. He was an enigma, she decided. She knew there were things about himself that he didn't like to talk about. She also knew he'd become much more open with her as their relationship had progressed. Closing her eyes, she sighed. *Please call, Cade*, she thought. *I need you!*

A Weakness For Chocolate

Morgandy Caye

CHAPTER FIFTEEN

Cade propped three pillows against the headboard of his bed and leaned back with a sigh. He ran his hand over his taut belly and the broad, tanned expanse of his chest. His shirt hung over a nearby chair. An open pizza box lay next to him. One slice of greasy pepperoni stuck to a glob of congealed cheese in the center of the box. He'd picked up the pie on his way back from the lawyer's office that afternoon, and along with a few beers from a cold six-pack, it had made his dinner. Three cans of the brew stood in a puddle of condensation on the night table next to him. They were warm now, and anyway, he'd had his fill. The television droned across the room. A cop show re-run that he knew he'd seen on at least two other occasions had him reaching for the remote.

As he scanned the cable offerings, his thoughts turned to Sage. He'd give her a call, he decided. He was excited to share his news with her. She's probably home from Denver by now, he thought. Picking up the phone, he dialed her familiar number and waited for the ring. He imagined her walking across the living room and into the kitchen to pick up. He also imagined that she'd be wearing one of those delicious confections women called a nightie; maybe a pink one, he speculated. The phone kept ringing as his thoughts drifted.

"Hello?" A deep, masculine voice answered sleepily. Cade was confused. Had he dialed the wrong number? He hesitated, thinking about hanging up.

"Hello?" The voice repeated.

"Is Sage there?" He finally forced a response.

"Yeah," the man's voice continued. "But I'm pretty sure she's asleep. Could I take a message?"

Not sure who he was speaking with, Cade finished with, "No thanks, I'll try again tomorrow," and hung up.

*　　　　*　　　　*　　　　*

Wondering if that had been the Sage's mystery man, Don returned to the sofa and fell instantly into a deep sleep.

*　　　　*　　　　*　　　　*

With his heart pounding, Cade hung up. Why was a guy answering Sage's phone? He didn't know what was going on, but he had a sick feeling in his belly. His thoughts were in turmoil as he tried to focus on a baseball game. He took a few deep breaths, and several minutes later, when his heart had stopped pounding and he was thinking more rationally, he told himself there was probably a very simple explanation. He didn't know what it was, but he thought he knew Sage, and she'd been decent and honest in the short time he'd known her. She deserved the benefit of the doubt. On that thought, Cade pulled his clothes off, and after a hot shower he slid between the cool sheets on the hotel bed and drifted off to sleep with the game still playing in the background.

*　　　　*　　　　*　　　　*　　　　*

The next morning, Sage awoke to the smell of coffee and the sound of her father rustling around out in the kitchen. She snuggled back under the warm covers and breathed deeply, relishing the warmth and comfort of her own bed after being away. After a few minutes, the freshly-brewed coffee aroma prevailed, and she dragged herself out of bed. As she trudged past her dresser, she caught sight of her reflection in the mirror and decided a stop in the bathroom was in order. Her hair showed definite signs of bed head, and her puffy eyes could use a splash of cold water.

As she walked down the hall, her Dad stuck his head around the corner.

"Hey, sleepyhead!" he grinned. Her dad was always so cheerful in the morning. Sage remembered how annoyed she used to get at his early morning good moods. Now, she just smiled back.

"Good morning, Dad. Coffee smells great! I'll be out in a minute. Did you find the banana muffins in that bag next to the microwave?"

"Muffins?" Don's voice picked up a beat. "I love banana muffins!"

"I know. That's why I made them!" Sage laughed as she walked into the bathroom, pulling the door closed behind her.

   *   *   *   *

  Cade woke to the smell of stale pizza and essence of motel, with the rumble of traffic outside. Despite his impersonal surroundings, his stomach fluttered with excitement. Today he took possession of the ranch, his ranch! The paper work had been completed yesterday, and Ruth Jamison had handed him the keys before he left the office. Now he couldn't wait to drive back out there and really look around.

  He grabbed a breakfast burrito and coffee at a fast food drive-through, and then headed back down the familiar road to the ranch. He spent the better part of the day there taking in every nuance of the place. He looked again through the house and outbuildings, then drove around the pastures, checked the windmills, and did a quick once-over of the fence lines. He made mental notes of the supplies he'd need to get things back in shape. Late in the afternoon, his rumbling belly led him back to town where he found a mom and pop café that served up a half-pound hamburger with a mountain of fries.

  After his meal, Cade stopped at the local bank where the account was kept in which Sam had left the cow money. He figured there was enough to buy about fifty cows now, and still have some for feed this winter as well as for the repairs needed around the ranch. Sam had run about eighty cows, and Cade would build up to that, but he didn't want to over-extend himself before he even started. He could rent out the smaller pasture south of the hayfield, and the money from that would help him get through the first year until he had a calf crop to sell. Cade got his account book, some checks to use until the ones he ordered came in, and enough money to get back home. When he'd left, it had been the end of the pay period and he hadn't had much cash on hand.

That night, Cade called Lloyd and told him he'd be back the next day in time for the sale.

"I'm glad to hear from you," Lloyd admitted. "I was getting a little worried."

"I should have called sooner," Cade's tone was apologetic. "I've just had a lot going on. Anyway, I'll be there in time for work."

"Okay," Lloyd agreed. "See ya then."

Cade said goodbye and put the phone back in its cradle. Next he punched in Sage's number, but this time the phone rang and rang. No answer. *Oh well*, Cade told himself, *I'll be in Hope tomorrow.* He couldn't wait to see her again; couldn't wait to tell her about the ranch. He had something now; he was somebody. Thanks to Sam he had something to offer a special woman like Sage.

*   *   *   *

After breakfasting with her Dad, Sage walked with him to the suburban.

"You take good care of Grandma," Sage advised, giving
Don a hug before he climbed into the SUV. "I'll try to come out in a few weeks and see how she's doing."

"We'd like that, honey," Don's voice was comforting to her. "You know you're always welcome."

"Maybe Grandma'll be ready to come home then," Sage suggested. "I can bring her back."

"I know she'd love that," Don conceded. He waved as he backed out of Sages drive and pulled away. She watched him drive off, and then went back inside and got ready to bake pies. Tomorrow was sale day, and the show must go on.

Sage cranked up sixties music on her radio, opened the windows to let the warm summer breeze float in, and commenced rolling pie crusts. Even the catchy beat of the music pounding in her ears couldn't keep her thoughts from straying to Cade. *Why hadn't he called*, she kept asking herself. She'd thought of a thousand excuses for him; she wondered what the real one would be. She felt so angry and hurt now, that she wasn't sure she even wanted to hear it!

Later that afternoon, Sage loaded her car with pies, salad, roast beef, and the rest of the groceries and cruised the short distance to the café. Pulling up next to the front door, she braked, turned off the engine, and climbed out of her car. Hearing the lock click as she turned her key, she pulled the heavy glass door open, wedged a rock under the corner, and began to unload the food.

"How about a hand there, Sage?" Lloyd's approach startled her. For a second, she'd thought it was Cade, and then chided herself for the disappointment.

"Sure thing! I'd love some help." She injected a note of cheerfulness into her voice. Sage reached into the car, pulled out a tray of hamburger patties, and turned to walk into the café. Lloyd raised his eyebrows at her preoccupied expression, but Sage didn't notice. She was too busy remembering the other time she'd brought food for a sale. Cade had helped her carry in the load, and then she'd fixed a cinnamon roll for him. Just a few weeks ago; they'd come a long way in their relationship since that conversation in the café, or at least she'd thought so, but apparently she'd been wrong. It seemed to Sage that as long as she was around in person so sex was an option, Cade had been attentive. He'd acted like he cared, but obviously, for him, it had only been sex. Sage felt her eyes tear up as she opened the refrigerator door with one finger and slid

123

the burgers on a middle shelf. She kept her face hidden as she wiped the moisture away before turning to face Lloyd again.

"Are you expecting a big sale tomorrow?" She feigned interest as she walked to the car for another load.

"About 600 head," Lloyd informed her as she walked past him. "Not bad for a summer sale."

"Not bad at all," she agreed as she stepped out the door for another load.

CHAPTER SIXTEEN

Heat emanated from the grill, causing tendrils of damp curls to loosen from Sage's ponytail and stick to the sweat on her forehead. She worked in subdued silence, flipping burgers and manning the fryer as the waitresses laid order after order on the counter beside her. The waitresses bustled around the busy café taking orders and chatting with old friends. The noise level increased as farmers and ranchers filed in and found seats at tables with their friends and neighbors. A few women dotted the group; most dressed in jeans and boots like their husbands.

Sage forced herself to focus on her work. She was determined not to keep checking for Cade. She'd been dreading seeing him. She felt angry and scared, and so very hurt. She'd gone over and over in her mind possible scenarios. Would he ignore her? Act like nothing was wrong? Apologize? And how would she respond? She tried to concentrate on her work, filling orders methodically, forcing a smile when her waitresses and customers peeked into the kitchen to offer a greeting or a teasing comment.

Some minutes later, Sage sensed someone behind her. She started and turned quickly. Cade stood at the kitchen door, a tentative smile gracing his handsome face.

"Hey baby."

Sage felt stunned. His presence took her breath away. She'd nearly forgotten how intensely he affected her, how his chocolate brown eyes melted her insides into a warm pool that settled in her lower belly. She breathed deeply, and then turned back to the grill.

"Hey stranger," she hoped her voice sounded casual. "Long time no see." She kept her back to him. She knew her face would give away the turmoil she felt inside.

"Too long," he said. "I missed you."

Sage felt the anger and hurt well up inside her and spill over. "Missed me so much I only heard from you once in two weeks?" She knew her voice sounded bitter. "Seems like you must have been pining away for me."

"I know I have some explaining to do," he confessed. "but now isn't the time."

"Apparently the last two weeks weren't the time either," Sage heard the sarcasm lacing her voice.

"We have some things to settle here," Cade's eyes bore into her back. "I'll be lookin' you up later, Sage."

"I'll look at my calendar and see if I have time to see you." She turned in time to see a flash of his faded, denim shirt as he left the small kitchen.

*　　　*　　　*　　　*

Sage struggled through the day in a fog of emotion. She was unaware of the worried looks she got from her waitresses, Ellie, Helen and Shirley. The three older women watched over her like mother hens. Finally, after the last customer was gone and the cleaning was in progress, Ellie stepped into the kitchen and found Sage with her hands in a sink full of soapy water, tears streaming down her face.

"Why honey! What's wrong?" Ellie put an arm around Sage, and to Sage's dismay she completely lost it. Sage turned into Ellie's warm embrace and wept openly. "My goodness, Sage! What happened?"

Between sobs, Sage managed to confess that she was upset about Cade.

"I was gone for two weeks, and my grandma was so sick, and he didn't even call me to see how she was, or how I was. I thought we had something special, and now I can see how wrong I was. I just feel so stupid!" Her sobs had subsided, but her breath still came hard.

"Sweetie," Ellie began. "Sometimes we womenfolk just don't know what men are thinking. Does he have an explanation?"

"He says he does, but right now I don't even want to hear it. I feel like he's duped me already! I thought he truly cared about me, but obviously I was wrong!"

"Sounds like you need some time to think and get yourself lined out? Am I right?" Ellie gave Sage's shoulder a squeeze. "How about you come home with me for the weekend?" Sage had spent a few weekends with the Clements's before. Their ranch lay along the Republican River valley just across the border in Nebraska. Its secluded beauty seemed like a perfect retreat for Sage and her raw feelings. She needed time to think without worrying that Cade would show up at her house wanting to talk. She still wasn't ready to see him.

"Thanks, Ellie," she accepted. "That sounds like just what I need right now." Sticking her hands back in the sink, she gave her friend a tremulous smile. "Let's get finished up here and I'll run home and grab some clothes."

"Great!" Ellie smiled. "You know we love having you."

*   *   *   *   *

After loading the last semi with cattle and wrapping things up with Lloyd, Cade went home for a quick shower. Standing in the steamy cubicle, hot water pelting his back, Cade thought again about Sage's reaction in the café. He'd been rolling it around in his mind all afternoon. Her sarcasm had really surprised him. He hadn't expected her to be angry, although in hindsight he could understand her feeling neglected. He wasn't used to women, he realized. Oh, he'd had his share of flings over the years, but he'd never felt about a woman the way he felt about Sage.

He toweled off, pulled on his newest pair of levis and a clean chambray shirt, then slid his boots on at the door. He drove to Sage's house and was dismayed to see inky blackness behind every window. He got out anyway, walked up to the door and rang the bell. The sound echoed hollowly in the empty house. Damn it! Where was she? He thought back to that afternoon; to the tightening he'd felt in his belly when he'd looked in the kitchen doorway and seen her standing there, her back to him. He could still picture the curls that had escaped her ponytail clinging to her damp neck, and her white tank top molding to her figure in the humid heat of the kitchen.

He rang the bell again, knowing as he did so that it was a futile gesture. Slowly he turned and walked back to his truck, climbed inside, and sat slumped over the wheel. The hollow emptiness in his belly threatened to overtake him. After a few minutes, he started the engine and drove back home. He wasn't sure he could face the emptiness of his place, but he didn't know where else to go. He lay on the sofa and stared blankly at the television until he finally drifted to sleep sometime after 3:00 in the morning.

Sage followed Ellie home from the sale barn. The winding gravel road meandered along a creek bottom, then climbed over rolling hills until, about fifteen miles from town, it ended at the Clements Ranch. Sage marveled at the beauty of the place. Its homey simplicity drew her like a bee to brightly colored flowers. She always felt welcome and comfortable when she stayed with Ellie and Jack. In some ways, they reminded her of her grandparents, and the ranch where she'd visited while she was growing up.

She helped Ellie prepare a simple meal of grilled chicken and vegetables. Jack joined them, and they ate on the screened in porch while enjoying the warm evening sunshine.

"You're quiet tonight," Ellie looked at Sage affectionately. "You have a lot on your mind, don't you?"

"Yeah," Sage forced a smile. "It's just been a long day; a long couple of weeks for that matter."

"How's your Grandma doing, by the way?" John piped up.

"She's good," Sage said, relieved the attention had turned away from her. "She'll be home in a couple weeks. The doctor wanted her to stay there for checkups."

"She's a feisty one!" Ellie chuckled. "I'm sure she'll be back to her old self quickly." They all laughed, and Ellie stood up and began to pick up the dirty dishes. Sage stood to help, but Ellie stopped her.

"You've done enough dishes for today," she explained. "Jack can help me, can't you honey?" She winked at him.

129

"Sure thing," Jack stood and picked up the serving platter.

"I think I'll take a walk before it gets dark," Sage decided. "I love to walk out here. The scenery is gorgeous!"

"Go ahead, honey," Ellie encouraged her. "A nice walk will help you sleep better tonight."

Sage pushed the screen door open and stepped out onto the concrete sidewalk. She breathed deeply of the evening air, her senses assailed by the rich smells of grass and trees and earth and animals. She felt some of the tension leave her body as she headed off across the yard. Finding her pace, she walked easily along a grassy path that followed the fence line of a small pasture that lay between the Clements' homestead and the main road.

Her thoughts quickly turned to Cade. She wondered what he was doing, wondered how he'd reacted when he found out she wasn't at home. Maybe he didn't even go over to see, she argued with herself, but deep down she knew that wasn't true. She could tell when he came into the sale barn kitchen that he'd really wanted to see her and talk to her. She imagined him walking up to her little house and ringing the bell, maybe even peering in to the dark windows looking for her. Doubt crept into her head. Had she made a mistake by coming out here? Was she running away from him? Hiding? She walked on, lost in thought, trying to analyze her feelings about Cade Lofton and what had happened between them over the past few weeks.

She'd fallen hard for him. She knew that. And she'd been so sure he felt the same. Maybe she'd misjudged, but she didn't think so. Especially after today, after the look on his face when she'd said she would see if she had time to talk to him. The hurt and confusion on his face made her regret the words. Remembering that look on his face made her question everything; her anger, his lack of communication, could she have misunderstood the situation?

Sage spent a restless night, and after a quick breakfast of Ellie's melt-in-your-mouth cinnamon rolls, she made her excuses, thanked Jack and Ellie for their hospitality, and drove slowly back to town. She was home by mid-morning, and was so glad to be in her own little house, alone with her thoughts. She opened the windows to let out the stuffy air, and started several sprinklers around the yard to nourish her parched plants that had withered in the summer heat.

A couple of hours later, after wandering around her house, trying to write, finally giving up, and thinking constantly about Cade, Sage decided maybe writing him a letter was the way to go. She figured if she took it over right away he would still be at work. She would stick it in his door and leave. She sat down at her computer and began typing, then decided this letter deserved to be hand-written. She got out her stationary, her favorite black gel pen, and started out

Dear Cade.

I'm sorry I was so rude yesterday. I'm feeling pretty upset about how things have been between us the last couple weeks. I know a lot has happened, but after how close we had been, I was surprised and disappointed when you didn't try to contact with me while I was in Denver. When I finally got home, I was so excited to see you again and you were gone. No explanation, just gone. I didn't know what to think, and I still don't. What do you want with me?

Sage

She folded the sheet of stationary and slipped it into a matching lavender envelope, then drove to Cade's house, praying under her breath that he wouldn't be home. She breathed a sigh of relief when she pulled up to his place and saw that his pickup wasn't there. Walking quickly up to the door, Sage grasped the envelope tightly. She pulled the screen door open and stuck her letter between the door and frame, letting the screen shut against it holding it in place. She turned to walk away and was half way down the steps when she heard the door open behind her. Sage froze in her steps, her chest tightening as she turned to look back. Cade was outlined in the open doorway, faded jeans hugging his slim hips, his chest bare.

"Running away?" his sarcastic tone stabbed at her.

"I didn't think you were home." Sage hated the tremble in her voice.

"Looks like you planned on me not being here?" Cade's face looked hard to Sage, cold and unyielding, the lavender envelope in his hand.

"I did," she admitted, squaring her shoulders. "I'm better at writing than I am at talking so I wrote you a letter."

Sage looked down and quickly wiped a tear from the corner of her eye. She hated it when she cried like this. She just didn't realize how hard it would be when she saw him.

Cade's heart melted when he saw her struggling not to cry.

"Baby," he coaxed, his tone soft now, "come in here and talk to me?" Cade reached out to her. Sage looked into his chocolate brown eyes and her insides melted like a chocolate chip in a cookie hot from the oven. Silently, she walked toward him, their eyes locked. When she climbed the wooden steps of his porch, he took her hand and pulled her inside. Sage heard the door shut behind her as she brushed past Cade. She inhaled deeply, the scent of him surrounding her. Vivid memories filled her head. She pictured them making love on the sofa, then snuggling there later with the light of the TV casting shimmering shadows on the walls. She could almost feel the heat of Cade's hard chest against her back, his arms holding her tightly as his soft breath whispered past her ear.

Cade's hand on her arm pulled her back into the present. She looked up at him.

"Tell me what's going on between us?" Sage's low voice pulled at something deep inside him. "I feel like we're playing a game, and I don't know the rules."

"What I feel for you is no game." The conviction in his voice reassured her. Her eyes were on his, their guarded expression demanding proof. "It's the realest thing I've ever felt." He looked down. "But I don't know the rules either. I've never felt this way before, never cared about someone the way I care about you.

"Me neither," Sage whispered. "Why didn't you call when I was in Denver? I thought you would. It made me feel like you didn't really care about me, like you just wanted me when I was available for sex." The words she'd been waiting to ask rushed from her. It wasn't at all like she'd planned. She'd rehearsed in her mind what she would say when she confronted him, and the lines in her mental dialogue never included the hurt that was apparent in her voice, or the trembling she felt in her lower lip. Her control was so tenuous that she turned away from him, not wanting him to see her weakness.

Her words hit Cade like a punch in the gut. *'How can she think that?'* He asked himself. He could see her trembling, but after the way she'd left last night when she knew he needed to talk to her, he held himself back. He'd felt so empty inside when she wasn't there. He was scared to reach out to her. Cade lowered himself onto the sofa, hugging a pillow to his belly.

"I thought about you every day," he began. "I wanted to talk to you, and know how you were doing."

"Then why didn't you call?" Sage's hurt was so apparent in her voice that Cade had to force himself to go on.

"I didn't know if your parents knew about me, or what they would think." He began. "I just hoped that you'd call me, and when you did it felt so good to hear your voice. I couldn't wait for you to get home." Hearing the explanation now, Cade knew it sounded lame. Despite how much he'd wanted to talk to her, he hadn't been able to bring himself to call. He knew if Sage's parents were aware of his background, they'd never allow their daughter to have anything to do with him.

"My parents know about you," Sage told him. "They have for a while now." She laughed softly, in a self-deprecating way. "Guess I should have known better than to tell them, huh?" she looked over to see Cade watching her, his eyes full of questions. "I felt stupid when you never called," she explained. "They must have been wondering why this guy who I had told them was so great never even bothered to call and see how I was."

"I'm sorry, Sage." Cade's deep voice trembled. "I do care about you...a lot"

"I thought you did," she began. "But then when I was going through such a difficult time, and you didn't seem to care, I started to doubt your feelings for me."

"Don't doubt them, baby." Cade looked at her with such longing, it was all Sage could do not to run into his arms.

"I'm sorry I did," she looked at him with tears running down her face. Cade stood and walked to her, pulling her into his arms. Sage pressed her cheek against Cade's chest as she held him tightly around the waist.

"I have a lot to learn about this relationship stuff, honey." Cade whispered against her hair. "Help me know what you need. I want to make you happy."

"I need you Cade. Just you," Sage's lips found his and the taste of him melted on her tongue like a candy bar left too long in the sun. Cade groaned deep in his throat as he molded Sage's lush body to his, one hand reaching down to cup her shapely bottom.

Being in Cade's arms like this made the past few weeks without him disappear. Sage felt the ball of hurt in her belly fade away as the warmth of his mouth molded her own. She moaned softly and parted her lips, eager to taste him. She felt his tongue gently trace her upper lip.

*   *   *   *   *

Later that night, ensconced in Cade's arms as they lay in soft warmth of his king-sized bed, Sage felt contented and safe. Sage told Cade about her time in Denver, and how frightened she'd been during her Grandma's illness. Cade described his busy week at the sale barn, how a load of young cattle from Montana had come in, and how so many of them had gotten sick from dust pneumonia. He and Lloyd had worked steadily doctoring them and checking them round the clock before they were healthy enough to be turned out to pasture.

"Where were you when I came home?" Sage finally got around to asking. "I came right over here to see you, and when I couldn't find you, I went to Lloyd, and he told me you'd taken off for a few days, and he didn't know for sure where you'd gone, just that you'd be back in time for the sale."

Cade turned to her and gathered her into his arms again.

"Yeah, I didn't know what was going to happen, so I didn't say much to Lloyd. I got this phone call from the past, and I had to go check it out."
Sage felt dread creeping back into her belly.

"So what happened?" She wasn't sure if she wanted know.

"Well, I got the most amazing news. Both good and bad, actually." He couldn't keep the emotion out of his voice.

"What?" She probed. "You sound like a kid at Christmas who isn't sure if he likes the gift Santa brought him."

"That's exactly how I feel," he admitted.

"What!" Sage declared, "Tell me already!"

Cade chuckled.

"I got a call from a lawyer last week. She lives in the town where I graduated from high school, Canyon Ridge Nebraska."

"And?" Sage prompted.

"And," Cade continued, "she told me some bad news and some good news."

"A mixed bag, huh?" Sage looked concerned.

"Yeah, definitely a mixed bag." Cade described his time working for Sam and Carol Taylor, and how they'd taken him under their wing and made him feel like their own. He didn't go in to his earlier life, his time in foster care after he'd lost both his parents. He knew he was leaving out important information, but he just couldn't bring himself to tell her. He couldn't face seeing the pity in her eyes.

"The lawyer, Ruth Coleman, told me Sam Taylor had died, and Carol had passed away several years before." Cade's voice trailed off.

"Oh no," Sage sympathized. "I'm so sorry Cade!"

"Yeah," Cade confessed. "I was pretty upset. They were some of the most wonderful people I've ever known. It came as quite a shock. Maybe it shouldn't have. I haven't kept in touch with them, but I always meant to go back and visit, I just hadn't made it yet."

"I know how that goes," Sage commiserated.

"But the good news is," Cade's voice filled with excitement, "that they left their ranch to me!"

"Their ranch?" Sage was stupefied. "They left you their ranch?"

"That's what I thought too," Cade told her. "I couldn't believe it. Sometimes I still think it's all a dream."

"What does that mean?" She asked. "Are you leaving here?"

"Well," Cade began, "yeah, I guess I am. I haven't told Lloyd yet."

"When?" Sage's voice sounded hollow, like the empty feeling in her tummy.

"In a few weeks. I haven't decided for sure. I'll definitely stay until after the horse sale. I know Lloyd is counting on me."

"Wow," Sage managed to utter. "I don't know what to say."

"Be happy for me, Sage," Cade pleaded. "Be happy for us. I want you to come see my place. It's what I've dreamed of; what I've been working for all my life."

"I am happy for you," Sage admitted. "I'm just not sure what it means for us."

"I'm not sure either," Cade replied. "But I know I don't want to lose you."

CHAPTER SEVENTEEN

Sage went home that night, despite knowing that Cade wanted her to stay. After his announcement that he would be leaving Hope, Sage felt so unsettled and confused that she needed time alone. She walked into her little house, felt its comforting atmosphere surround her, and went straight to her bedroom and her computer. She opened her writing program and clicked on a blank page. Sometimes writing helped her focus and get her thoughts in order. Sage began to type. Tiny black letters fell onto the screen like tear drops as she poured out her thoughts.

She felt a little better an hour later, when she shut down her computer and went out to her backyard. The scent of summer flowers wafted in the warm breeze as hummingbird moths hovered above the spiky centers of her coneflowers, dipping their long tongues into the stamens and drawing out the sweet nectar. Sage leaned back on the wicker loveseat, its flowered cushion soft beneath her. She took a deep breath and reminded herself what a blessing her home was, and how much she loved it here. She remembered how content she'd been before Cade Lofton entered her life. Sage felt a tear run down her cheek as she also thought about how happy and fulfilled she'd been during their first weeks together, and the emotional roller coaster since Grandma Nina's heart attack. It felt more like a lifetime than a few short weeks.

You've got to take stock of your life Sage, she told herself. Part of her wanted Cade to ask her to go with him, but another part of her craved the independence she had built in her life since coming to Hope. She loved being on her own, building her writing career and running the little café at the sale barn. She felt at peace here in Grandma Nina's house. She'd made it her own, filling it with the things she loved most, but little reminders of her Grandma were everywhere; knickknacks, crocheted pillow tops, doilies, and especially the plants and flowers in the yard, some of them heirlooms from Nina's mother that had been transplanted at the ranch, then uprooted and brought to town when Nina had left the homestead. They were still thriving under Sage's loving care. How could she leave all that behind? On the other hand, how could she let Cade go? All she had were questions. After a quiet stroll around the yard, her bare feet sinking into the cool night grass as she walked, Sage went into the house and crawled into her bed. She worried that sleep would be a long time coming, but the emotions that had been coiled in her belly for the past few weeks had drained her, leaving her deeply exhausted, and she fell into a restless sleep.

A distant pounding pulled Sage from a deep sleep the next morning. Her groggy mind wondered at first what the noise was, and then she realized someone was knocking on her door. She threw off her covers and grabbed her robe, pulling it on as she walked down the hallway to the front door. She peeked out the window, and saw Lloyd standing on her porch.

"Morning Lloyd," Sage greeted him sleepily as she opened the door. "You caught me in bed," Sage admitted.

"Well, it's only 7:30," Lloyd said sheepishly. "But I thought you'd be up."

"I usually would be," Sage reassured him. "I need to be. Don't worry about it. What can I do for you," she smiled.

"I wanted to finalize plans for the horse sale. Could you come over to the office about 9:00?"

"Sure," Sage agreed. "See you in a little while."

She closed the door behind him, and trudged back down the hall to the bathroom. Maybe a hot shower would wake her up.

An hour and a half later, Sage drug herself into the sale barn office. The shower hadn't helped. She still felt like she'd been through the ringer. She only hoped she looked better than she felt. She stopped short when she saw Cade sitting in the chair opposite Lloyd's desk, his black cowboy hat in his lap. Both men looked up when she stopped at the door. Her still damp hair curled around her face, and the faded denim shorts and pink t-shirt she'd donned suddenly seemed inadequate.

"Should I come back later?" Sage asked, feeling uncomfortable.

"No, it's okay," Lloyd reassured her. "Cade has been telling me about his inheritance. Sounds like quite an opportunity."

"Yes, it does," Sage agreed. "He told me last night." She sat down in the chair next to Cade, and he reached for her hand. Sage gave his fingers a quick squeeze, and then pulled her hand away. She couldn't quite bring herself to meet his eyes, even though she felt him staring at her, willing her to look his way.

She glanced at Lloyd and realized he was talking. Forcing herself to focus, Sage zeroed in on his voice. "...with only a week to go," Lloyd finished.

"Until what?" Sage blurted out.

"The horse sale," amusement tinged Lloyd's voice. "Are you with us, Sage?"

Flushing, Sage mumbled, "I am now."

"She had a short night," Cade explained. "We both did."

Lloyd smiled. "I'm sure talking about your inheritance made for a lot of conversation." Cade and Sage both just looked at him. "Well, back to the horse sale," Lloyd continued.

"I have nearly eighty head consigned so far," Lloyd shared. "I hope to have nearly one hundred counting the horses brought in on sale day."

"Sounds like a good sale," Cade interjected.

"Yes, it's shaping up to be well-worth our time." Excitement filled Lloyd's voice, making Sage smile.

"How many people should I plan to feed?" Sage questioned.

"I'm thinking around 300," Lloyd speculated. "I'm going to have the sale advertised on radio and in the local paper, as well as a regional paper." He continued, "Since we're doing a hog roast, what will be the easiest way to go for serving that many people? A buffet line? I've got a guy lined up to cook the meat. He does it as a sideline business."

"I think a buffet line would work well," Sage pointed out. "There's no way we could easily take orders from that large a group. It would take way more waitresses than my little bunch!"

Cade laughed and leaned forward slightly to give her leg a squeeze. "I expect Ellie could get the job done," he joked.

"If anyone could, it'd be Ellie," Lloyd agreed.

Sage blushed, glad her legs were hidden behind the desk. Her senses were focused on Cade's hand against her skin. His thumb drew lazy circles against her thigh as he talked to Lloyd. His touch distracted her, and she struggled to stay focused on the conversation.

"Well, I guess that's all for now," she heard Lloyd finish. "I'm heading to the Thompson pasture to work on the windmill," he informed Cade. "Why don't you take the two-horse trailer, and go check on that steer we doctored for pink-eye a couple days ago. I want to make sure he's getting better." Lloyd stood and headed out the door. Sage stood quickly and started to follow him, but Cade took her arm and pulled her onto his lap. The door slammed shut behind Lloyd, leaving them alone in the building.

"Where you goin' sweetie?" He pulled her close. She looked into the chocolate-brown depths of his eyes and saw the questions there, questions she had no answers for.

"I can't answer your questions," she whispered.

"I didn't ask any."

"I see them in your eyes," she admitted.

"How about we forget the questions for now?" Cade smiled a little. "Everything's so new for us. Let's take a day at a time and see what happens. Can you handle that?" He hugged her and felt her nod against his chest. "Give me a kiss, and then I'd better get to work."

Sage lifted her face and pressed her mouth softly against his. She couldn't help letting the tip of her tongue slide between her lips for a taste. Cade groaned, and their contact deepened, his tongue meeting hers. The taste of him filled her, and in the back of her mind she heard an engine as Lloyd drove by the office heading out to repair the windmill.

"You're making it hard to leave, baby," Cade whispered.

"Uh huh," she smiled, looking up at him with a twinkle in her blue eyes. "I missed you."

"You're the one who wanted to go home last night, remember?" He teased.

"Now I don't want to go home," Sage's voice melted into a whimper as Cade cupped her breast through her thin t-shirt. Her stretchy, knit bra offered little protection. She felt her nipple tighten under his palm. He felt it too, and lifted his hand, using his fingers to trace lightly around her swollen bud. She arched against him and pressed her mouth to his again. Under her hip, she felt his cock stiffening. She couldn't resist rocking gently against it.

"You're a naughty girl," Cade's voice was deep with hunger as he lifted his mouth from hers. "Turn around and face me so you can take your punishment."

"Punishment?" Sage giggled, rising from his lap to turn and straddle his legs before sitting down again. He put his hands on her hips and pulled her forward until the juncture of her thighs was nestled over the bulge in his jeans.

"Mmmm," Sage murmured. "Feels to me like you might be the naughty one!"

"We'll see," Cade whispered before leaning down to take a swollen nipple into his hot mouth. He sucked and bit lightly at it through her clothes, making a wet place on the fabric over her breast. He then gave the other nipple equal treatment. Sage arched her back, lifting her ample breasts toward him. She groaned and felt herself rocking against his lap. He lifted her t-shirt then, and unclasped the front-hook of her pink bra. Her breasts bounced free, and Cade stared with appreciation.

"Mmm, baby, you like showing me your big breasts, don't you?" He reached up and took her erect nipples between his fingers, twisting and stretching them gently.

"Ahh," was all Sage could manage, her senses in a turmoil of arousal.

"Are you wet for me?" He knew she was. He could feel the heat of her arousal against the front of his jeans. Taking a nipple into his mouth again, Cade sucked rhythmically as he slid his hand under the loose waistband of her cotton shorts. "No panties?" He queried. "You're even naughtier than I thought."

She felt Cade's fingers slide across her pubic mound. His middle finger slid between her swollen sex lips and found the slick heat, circling her swollen center.

"You make me naughty," she whimpered. "I melt when you touch me."

"Yes," he agreed. "I feel you melting, and I melt too. Unfasten my jeans, Sage," he directed, continuing to stroke her, slipping a finger into her tightness. She fumbled with his belt and zipper, but finally worked them free. Her fingers probed the opening in his boxers, feeling the silky hardness of his erection. Circling it with her thumb and forefinger, she lifted it through the slit in his shorts.

"Feels like you're going to be melting before long yourself, cowboy," she teased. Cade groaned as she grasped his arousal and slid her soft hand up and down the shaft, squeezing and tugging gently right below the rim.

"I'm going to melt inside you," Cade whispered hoarsely. He lifted Sage, and she held the leg band of her shorts to the side and guided him to her swollen opening. She felt his engorged cock stretching her as he slowly lowered her onto his lap again. When he was fully embedded inside her, his hands once again went to work on her magnificent breasts, toying with them expertly as she began to rock and swivel on his lap, her rotating hips causing her swollen center to rub at the base of his erection.

After only seconds, Sage felt her orgasm building, and as it washed through her she cried out, oblivious to the fact that they were in a public building. Cade felt her hot wetness contracting around him, and he did as he'd promised, shot his essence into her, melted into her.

"Ah, Sage," he whispered. "I can't believe what you do to me."

"I think I'm falling in love with you," she whispered as she leaned against him. He just held her tightly, his breathing slow and even.

CHAPTER EIGHTEEN

The day of the horse sale dawned bright and hot. As she drove to the sale barn with her car full of food, Sage squinted behind her sunglasses at the glaring prairie sun beating down on her windshield. Already the pale blue sky shimmered with heat waves. This was her second trip from home. She'd spent the previous day shopping and cooking, and that evening, she and Cade, along with Lloyd and a couple other guys who worked on sale days, had set up the tables. Four long rows of plywood planks sat atop saw horses that were sandwiched between rows of hay bales for seating. Huge cottonwood trees shaded the eating area, which was located in the parking lot near the café.

Sage backed her car up to the café door and began carrying in food. Glancing at the door to Lloyd's office, she thought about Cade making love to her in the chair. Thank God no one had walked in. When Cade touched her she forgot everything else. They hadn't had time to talk about his move yet. Between the horse sale preparations and some illness among the pasture cattle, Cade had been swamped. She'd been too busy to even think about it, what with cooking for the sale. Cade had come over to her place last night, and after a late supper of roast beef sandwiches they'd fallen asleep in front of the television, spooning together on the wide sofa.

Sage worked steadily for an hour, until the waitresses arrived and pitched in to get the serving line set up. The meal would be dished up buffet-style from two long tables set up in the café.

"How's Nina doing?" Ellie called across the café as she carried bottles of ketchup to the buffet tables.

"Great," Sage announced. "I called her this morning, and she can't wait to get back home. She says mom and dad are treating her like an invalid, and she can't stand it much longer!" Laughter filled the café.

"I'm glad to hear she's sounding like her old self!" Shirley chuckled.

"Me too," relief was evident in Sage's voice. "I can't wait to have her back here."

The women worked steadily, their laughter and conversation occasionally drowned out by the rattle of pickups and trailers pulling into the sale barn grounds. A horse sale was always a popular event in Hope, with more people there to watch than to make a purchase. Lloyd had stopped in earlier that morning, and told Sage that he'd gotten a good line of horses consigned. He was especially excited about the good-quality group of working ranch horses that would be sold. Sage had laughed at him. He was like a kid whose birthday party was coming up.

Sage stood behind a table stirring brown sugar into a big roaster of baked beans. Next to her, Ellie was arranging a huge bowl of homemade potato salad in an insulated tub filled with ice.

"This potato salad looks delicious, as always," Ellie complimented Sage's cooking skills. "With everything going on, have you had time to do any writing?" She queried.

"I always make time for that," Sage replied, emphasizing the always, "but lately it's been a bit harder. I write some everyday, but it isn't always good writing," she laughed. "Between Grandma's problems and my situation with Cade, feeling creative is a challenge sometimes."

"What is your situation with Cade," Ellie questioned. "If you don't mind my asking, that is?"

"Well," Sage hesitated.

"It's okay if you don't want to talk about it," Ellie's voice was reassuring.

"It isn't that," Sage confessed. "I just don't know what the answer is."

"How so?" The older woman looked at Sage with concern.

"Cade just found out he got a nice inheritance, a ranch, up in Nebraska. So he'll be moving there soon." Sage glanced at Ellie, worry filling her eyes. "I just don't know what that means for us, or even what I want it to mean."

"I know how scary it is when the clear answers aren't there," Ellie was a good listener, something Sage had discovered early on in their friendship. Sage always liked the way Ellie seemed to understand her problems, and offer help without seeming bossy or judgmental. "When Jack asked me to marry him, I was just out of high school. I'd always thought I wanted to get out of Hope for a few years at least, work in the city or go to college, but I also felt like ultimately I wanted to spend my life on a ranch, and spend it with Jack. We'd dated for two years before that, you know." Ellie's voice lowered. "It was scary for me, making that choice to get married, giving up on some of my plans so that others would happen. I can't tell you what the right choice is, Sage. For the most part I've been pretty happy, but there have been a few times when I wondered if I made the right decision, wondered what I'd missed."

"I think everyone feels that way at one time or another," Sage agreed with her. "Cade and I are at such an early stage in our relationship. In some ways, it's moved so far so fast, and in others it's really new. Until this thing with the inheritance came up, Cade hadn't told me the whole story of his childhood," Sage's voice filled with emotion. "That's a pretty big deal. It makes me wonder what else he is hiding from me."

"I can see how it would," Ellie commiserated. "But I can also see how a person might feel scared to share that. Maybe he had a bad experience and he was hurt by it?"

"I think that's true," Sage relayed some of what Cade had shared with her. "He didn't say a whole lot, but it sounded like a not-so-good situation."

"Maybe he thinks that reflects badly on him?" Ellie voiced her thoughts. "Often, people don't like to admit they've been treated badly. They feel somehow to blame for it."

"That's crazy!" Sage blurted out. Did Cade think that? Was he ashamed? Questions raced through her mind.

"I know," Ellie continued. "I'm just speculating here, but what little I know Cade Lofton, he seems like a good man, an honorable one."

"For the most part, I think so too," Sage agreed. "It's just that I've only known him for a couple months now, and that isn't very long. I don't want to be naïve, to just believe everything he says and ignore what he doesn't, and then get hurt for it."

"Yes," Ellie responded, sticking spoons into the potato salad. "Caution is good, but sprinkle on a bit of courage too. You have a good head on your shoulders, Sage. Listen to your intuition."

"Should I start slicing the cakes?" Shirley interrupted as she walked up to Sage and Ellie. "Oh, sorry, I didn't mean to butt in." She flushed.

"It's fine, Shirley," Sage reassured her. "And yes, you should definitely start slicing the sheet cakes. I want to have them ready to dish up as people go through the line. It'll be smoother if they get their dessert along with their meal, instead of having to come through the line again."

"That's what I thought too," Shirley announced, heading for the cakes with knife in hand.

*   *   *   *

The horse sale went smoothly, lasting well past dark. By the time the last horse was loaded out to go home with its new owner, it was nearing 11:00 p.m. Sage sat at one of the long tables under the cottonwood trees, her head lying on her arms. Her meal had been an overwhelming success, and had run easily with the help of her experienced waitresses. By the time they had finished serving and cleaning up, it had been late afternoon, and the temperature by that time had soared well into the nineties. She and her waitresses had been decidedly wilted by the time their work was done. They sat in the shade, eating plates filled with what little had been left of the barbecue meal while they talked about the day and who had been there and what had been said or overheard.

Sage smiled to herself when she recalled the shocked expression on Shirley's face when Helen had related the news that Cheryl Parker was pregnant again.

"Again!" Shirley has gasped. "Is this six or seven?"

"Seven I believe," Helen informed her.

"My gosh," Shirley exclaimed. "Can you imagine trying to take care of that many kids?"

They'd all agreed that they couldn't imagine it, although Helen herself had four children, which Sage thought was a pretty big family.

The three older women had gone home soon after they finished eating, and Sage had headed in to the auction ring to watch some of the horse sale. She had always loved the horses at her grandparent's ranch, and spent many happy hours riding when she visited them. She sat back, tired and contented as horses went through the ring. Cade stood near the auction block, taking bids as the auctioneer sing-songed back and forth between bidders. She had watched him, taking in his lean, muscular build and strong face. He'd seen her looking and winked. Sage blushed, and winked back.

After a while the bright lights and noise of the auction had started giving her a headache, and Sage had wandered out to the tables, sitting in the cool darkness. Crickets chirped and she could hear, faintly, the back and forth sounds of bidders responding to the auctioneer's call.

That's where Cade found her. He looked in the café, and wondered briefly if she'd gone home until he saw her car still parked where it had been that morning. He walked outside, and after letting his eyes adjust to the darkness, he made out her shape sitting at one of the long tables near a huge cottonwood tree.

"Hey baby," he called softly. "You ready to go home?"
Sage lifted her head and turned in his direction.
"Whose home?"
"Whose home do you wanna go to?" he asked.
"Mine," she answered, "but only if you go with me."

"I was hoping you'd invite me," he chuckled. Taking her hand, Cade led Sage to her car, then walked to his truck, started it up, and followed her the short distance to her place.

*   *   *   *

Sage watched the morning sunlight pushing the smudgy darkness out of her bedroom. Cade was asleep next to her, his breathing soft and rhythmic. She lay still, enveloped in a warm pocket of body heat, hers and Cade's. They'd arrived home late the night before, exhausted from the long horse sale day, and fallen into bed after a quick shower. It was the first night they'd spent together that they hadn't made love. She wasn't disappointed, only making an observation; having him here felt right and comfortable and safe. Sage snuggled back down, hugging a pillow to her chest, and let her eyes close again.

When she woke an hour later, it was to the feel of Cade's hand sliding from her hip to her waist. The room glowed with bright morning sun, and the breeze coming through the window was already warm.

"Good morning," Sage murmured, rolling toward Cade. Her eyes took in his sleepy appearance. The chocolate brown of his eyes peeked from beneath half-closed lids lined with thick lashes. His mussed hair looked incredibly sexy to her. She giggled as his hand slid along her rib cage, and he smiled wickedly.

"Your even ticklish early in the morning," he teased.

"Your even naughty early in the morning," Sage laughed as his fingers walked determinedly up her sides, and then slid to cup her naked breasts.

"I'm not ticklish there!" She protested, but her resistance faded quickly as his fingers began their magic.

Later, they sat at her kitchen table devouring omelets filled with crispy bacon and shredded sharp cheddar, and washing it down with steaming cups of coffee made from freshly ground beans.

"You're the goddess of cooking," Cade announced with appreciation as he took another bite of buttery toast.

"What else am I the goddess of," she questioned, her eyes sparkling with mischief.

"Well," Cade began. "You're definitely the goddess of gardening."

"And?"

"And?" Cade laughed. "Based on your performance this morning, you've got my vote for the goddess of sexiness."

"You think?" She smiled. "You make me feel sexy," Sage admitted. "I didn't know it could be like that."

"Me either," Cade agreed. "I think it depends on the person your with."

"So you like being "with" me?" She probed.

"I crave it. But you already knew that, and not just for the sex." Cade shifted uncomfortably. He wasn't used to talking about how he felt. She just looked at him, waiting.

"You're not going to let me off the hook here, are you?" He grinned at her, his discomfort apparent.

"No."

"I like talking to you, watching you work, just being with you. It feels right to me, like this is how my life is supposed to be."

"I feel that way too," Sage agreed. "I'm just not sure how your inheritance will affect us. I like my life here, my house, my garden, being near grandma. My job at the café works out perfectly with my writing." Sage sighed. "But I like being with you too. I hate the idea of you being so far from me."

"Life can't ever be easy, can it?" Cade asked. "How about if you come with me this weekend and see my place. I don't know if it'll change anything, but I want you to see it. The ranch means a lot to me, and so do you. We'll figure out something. I don't want to lose you, Sage."

"I don't want you to lose me either." She grinned and leaned across the little table to give him a quick kiss before she started cleaning off the table.

CHAPTER NINETEEN

Sage stared silently out the window of Cade's pickup as they drove toward Canyon Ridge. The terrain hadn't changed much since they left Hope. Rolling hills covered with buffalo grass and yucca plants stretched between wide valleys dotted with farms. Fields of corn and alfalfa stretched between the farmsteads, and center pivot sprinklers provided the water that made the valleys green and lush. A creek lined with cottonwoods and elms meandered down the valley, and Sage glanced down through her window as the highway crossed over a fork of the creek to see if it held water. A thin, muddy stream moved sluggishly between banks lushly overgrown with weeds and grass.

"I think I've been through Canyon Ridge once," Sage reminisced. "I was staying with grandpa and grandma for the summer, I must have been about twelve. Grandpa was buying a corn planter from a guy there, and I rode with him to pick it up."

"Do you remember what it was like?" Cade glanced at her, wondering at her earlier quietness. He was glad she was talking now. The silence made him nervous for some reason he couldn't quite pinpoint.

"Not much," she continued. "I remember it seemed like a big town compared to Hope, and we ate lunch at a drive-in. Grandpa let me get a chocolate malt to go with my hamburger. Grandma always thought ice cream should be dessert, so she wouldn't have let me get a malt. I remember grandpa winked at me, like he was letting me get away with something naughty." Sage laughed, thinking about her grandpa's twinkling blue eyes. He had a streak of mischief, and she thought of Grandma Nina good-naturedly scolding him on several occasions.

"I think my grandparents must have had a good marriage," she went on. "They always seemed to have fun together, and they talked a lot. I remember laying in bed in my room across the hall from theirs, and listening to the low murmur of their voices as I went to sleep."

"That must be a good memory," Cade encouraged her to tell him more.

"Tell me some of your memories," she asked tentatively. Cade hadn't talked too much about his childhood, and she wasn't sure how he felt about it.

"I remember sitting on the porch on summer evenings waiting for my Dad to get done working. Most nights, he got done around 7:00, and he'd walk up to the house and lift me up and swing me around. I can remember laughing and looking down at his face as he held me above him and turned in circles. He'd always say, what're you goin' to feed me tonight, Cade my boy? And I'd say, I'm the little boy, Daddy, you gotta feed me! And he'd laugh and set me down and say, well then, we'd better get into the house so I can figure out what to feed you!"

Sage watched the expression on Cade's face as he talked, saw the softness and warmth in his eyes as he thought about his father. She couldn't imagine how hard it must have been for a little boy to lose his dad, and to have no one else in the world to love him. Tears welled up in her eyes, and she glanced down before Cade could see.

"Your dad must have been wonderful," she said.

"Yeah," his voice was strained. "It was hell after his accident."

"I can't even imagine." Even now Sage couldn't imagine what it would be like to lose her parents. It had been awful enough when she thought she might lose her grandma!

"We're almost there," Cade said, effectively changing the subject. My place is north of town, and we'll be coming in on the east side. It'll give you a chance to see the town when we drive through."

"Great!" Sage smiled, her enthusiasm not completely feigned.

Canyon Ridge's downtown was lined with trees that shaded a nice selection of stores. Sage was impressed at the variety of shops, and the cleanliness of the community. It was certainly bigger than Hope, yet not so big as to be considered a city. A couple of blocks further, the business district gave way to a more residential area, and Cade turned North heading down a shady street lined with nice homes. Near the edge of town, he motioned to the right.

"That's the street my foster parents lived on."

"Did you ever go back to see them?" Sage wondered aloud.

"No way!" Cade's voice deepened with the intense dislike he felt for the people who had given him shelter and little else. "I have nothing good to say to them." He continued, "All they ever gave me was a roof over my head, barely enough food to eat, and the cheapest clothes they could find at second hand stores."

Sage heard the hatred in his voice.

"Sounds awful; I wouldn't go back there either."

"No, you wouldn't," Cade confirmed.

As they drove north of Canyon Ridge, leaving the tree-covered streets behind, Sage was still thinking about what Cade's life must have been like. She hoped someday he'd feel comfortable talking about it.

"How far is it from town?"

"About twelve miles," Cade replied. "It's a beautiful drive, especially in the spring and summer when things are green."

"It is," she agreed. "The country's a bit like Hope, but maybe more rocky. It's really pretty."

"Almost as pretty as you," Cade glanced at her with a grin, then chuckled when she blushed. "We're almost there," he announced. "The ranch is just over this hill."

Sage gasped when the ranch came into view. From a distance, it's ranch house with the broad porch, and the red barn surrounded by corrals looked neat and well-kept. It was only when they got closer that Sage could see it was a bit run-down. Still, it was a beautiful place.

"It's been empty for a while," Cade explained. "Sam's lawyer had minimal upkeep done, but it'll take some work to get it back to what it used to be." They pulled up in front of the house, and Sage stepped out of the truck. The yard was surrounded by a white picket fence, and with her gardener's eye Sage took in the enclosure. A redbud tree graced one corner, while a huge lilac bush filled another. She could imagine how awesome they looked in the spring blooming profusely.

"This yard has some possibility," she observed.

"You should have seen it when Carol was alive. She had a green-thumb like you." Cade imagined how lush the yard used to be, overflowing with color and texture, flowers that bloomed in spring, summer and fall.

"I wonder if some of her plants and bulbs are still here, just in hiding?" Sage wondered.

"Possible." Cade took her hand and pulled her toward the house. "Come on Miss Green Thumb, I want you to see the inside." Sage laughed and followed him, taking in the wide, shady porch and picturing a porch swing there.

"This would be perfect for a porch swing," she announced.

"Once again, you're right. Now come on in." Smiling, Cade unlocked the kitchen door and led the way.

*   *   *   *

On the way back to Hope, Cade and Sage talked endlessly about his ranch. He told her the plans he'd made, and described how the ranch had been run when Sam Tyler owned it. She threw out ideas about ways she'd seen improvements could be made. She loved seeing how excited Cade was about his inheritance; about this chance he'd been given. His excitement was contagious, and he obviously wanted her to be part of it. He cared about her ideas and about sharing it all with her.

They drove and talked, and the miles flew by, until Hope was in view. As they pulled up in front of Sage's house, her cell phone rang.

"Hello?" she answered. "Hi Dad." Nodding as she listened, Sage smiled at Cade. He sat, listening and rubbing her shoulder as she talked. After a short conversation, she disconnected and turned to him.

"Dad says Grandma has been released by the doctor and she wants to come home." Sage's voice was excited. "I told them I'd come get her."

"When will you go?" Cade inquired as they got out of the truck and headed up her front walk.

"Well, I know she'll be anxious to get home as soon as possible," Sage laughed.

"Since we don't have a sale this week, I suppose you could go tomorrow, huh?" Cade held the screen door open as Sage unlocked the inner door. She pushed the door open, then turned to face Cade.

"Any chance you could go with me?" she asked. "I'd like you to see where I grew up, and to have you meet my family. Would that bother you?"

"I suppose I'd be a little nervous," he grinned, "but I think I could handle it ok." Sage hugged him.

"Good," she said. "I think you could handle it just fine!"

"I'll have to make sure it's okay with Lloyd," he cautioned her, "but I doubt he'll care. Things aren't too busy around here this time of year."

"I hope he doesn't," Sage interjected. "Let's get something to eat. I'm starving!" She grabbed Cade's hand and led him into the kitchen.

CHAPTER TWENTY

The next morning they were headed for Denver. Lloyd had approved Cade being gone a couple more days. He didn't say anything, but he knew it was only a few more days until the younger man moved anyway. He had already been putting out feelers for a new hired man. The young couple drove in silence for a while, both tired from the previous day's long trip to Canyon Ridge. The crossed the rolling hills of northwestern Kansas and the broad plains of eastern Colorado.

"I always love the first glimpse of the mountains," Sage confessed. "I get a deep feeling of home. Besides my parents, the thing I miss most is the mountains. I could see them from my bedroom window."

"They are an awesome view," Cade agreed. "But even better is waking up to see you next to me."

"I like seeing you too." Sage smiled and took his hand.

They made small talk the rest of the way, and when they pulled into the driveway at Sage's childhood home, she honked and her mom came out the front door waving to them, grandma Nina was close behind. Sage jumped out of the car, hugging both women before turning to Cade, who stood beside the passenger door.

"How was your trip?" Renee Claremont inquired as she smiled welcomingly at the new arrivals.

"It was fine," Sage answered. "It feels good to be here." Turning to her grandmother, Sage continued, "Grandma! You look awesome!" She gave the older woman a long hug, then stepped back to look at her. "As good as new?" she asked.

"Back to my old self," Nina replied. "Can't wait to get back to my own house."

"I bet," Sage smiled. Then, grabbing Cade's hand, she turned.
"Mom, I'd like you to meet Cade Lofton,"

"Nice to meet you Mrs. Claremont." He took the hand Renee offered and shook it, then turned to Nina. "And to see you again too, Mrs. Claremont." The women laughed, and Sage was glad to see Cade charming them like he had her. His charm was so real. There was nothing artificial about Cade or how he treated people. Over the past few days, Sage had come to realize that about him. Even though he hadn't told her everything about his past, he'd opened up quite a bit, and she felt comfortable that in his own time he would talk to her about it all. It was a relief, but it still didn't solve her dilemma.

*   *   *   *   *

Sage showed Cade around her home, and then, after dinner, she drove him by her old school and the places in the neighborhood that evoked fond memories. They ended their tour with a stop at the Dairy Crème, a little mom and pop drive-in a couple blocks from the Claremont residence.

"Mom and Dad like you. I can tell." Sage announced as they sat at a picnic table licking vanilla ice cream cones.

"Oh yeah," Cade laughed. "How can you tell?"

"I just can," she grinned at him. "How could they not?"

"You're not exactly unbiased," He chuckled. "Watching you lick that cone gives me ideas," he whispered, his eyes turning dark chocolate with desire.

"Naughty ideas?" she whispered back.

"Very naughty," he confessed in a low voice. Sage laughed, and then made a point of licking her ice cream suggestively. Cade groaned.

"You're a very bad girl," he scolded her teasingly. "Lucky for you I like bad girls."

"I think this bad girl better get you home, cowboy," Sage "It's been a long day, and we'll have another tomorrow."

"I think you're right," Cade agreed, standing and reaching for Sage's hand. "Take me home, naughty girl."

      *   *   *   *

The next morning dawned clear and bright. The Rockies towered above the foothills, greeting the sun as it rose in the blue morning sky. After loading Grandma Nina and her things, Cade and Sage climbed in the car and headed east. Nina questioned Sage about the goings-on in Hope, about the outcome of the horse sale, and about how Sage's writing was coming along. She questioned Cade about his job, his background, and his political views. Sage thought he did a good job of satisfying the older woman's questions. She smiled inwardly, amused at her grandma's probing him for information. She hoped Cade was equally amused.

After a quick stop for sandwiches at a fast food outlet they were back on the road, and arrived in Hope by mid-afternoon. Sage drove to her grandmother's apartment first, and they helped her unload and get settled. The apartment was stuffy and stale smelling from being closed up, and the refrigerator was bare. Sage promised to go with Nina the next day to restock her cupboards, and then they could have lunch together and catch up. Nina invited Cade too, but he allowed as how he would be working and couldn't take a long lunch break. He smiled at Nina, who promptly melted into a simpering heap.

The next morning, Sage drove to pick up her grandmother with the bright prairie sun glaring in her eyes like a camera flash, even her sunglasses didn't help much. Whenever she drove through Hope, Sage enjoyed seeing the pretty, well-kept yards and neat homes. The late summer gardens were dotted with colorful petunias and snapdragons, their pastel colors reminding Sage of brightly died Easter eggs. She also saw rows of four-o'clocks, their trumpeted throats taking in the early light before closing for the day, only to open again when the sun began to set.

Well-manicured grounds surrounded Sunrise Village where Nina now lived. The carefully planted rows of marigolds and pansies were laid out in a grid-like fashion, much different from the wild profusion of flowers in Sage's cottage garden, and much different from the style of garden Nina herself had always favored, but pretty nonetheless. The building itself was constructed of golden-colored brick, and was laid out in an L-shape with apartments on both wings. Sage approached her grandmother's apartment from the outside, crossing her small, concrete patio to knock on the sliding door. Nina's taste in gardening showed in the hanging baskets and pots overflowing with bright flowers and trailing ivy that filled her patio. Sage noted that one of the neighbors must have watered them while Nina had been gone.

"Grandma?" Sage announced her arrival. "Are you up?" she continued in a teasing voice. Nina always prided herself on getting up with the roosters and getting her best work done in the morning.

"Of course I'm up," Nina's voice came from the bathroom, and she stuck her head around the corner, a makeup brush in hand. "You know better than to think I'd still be in bed!" she scolded Sage teasingly.

"Getting beautiful, I see," Sage grinned as she walked to the bathroom door then leaned against the frame and watched her grandma finish dabbing on blush.

"We aren't all as pretty as you first thing in the morning," Nina retorted. "Now where's my purse?" The older woman bustled around, gathering up her pocketbook, sunglasses and scarf. "I made a list last night. Now where is it?" She mumbled.

"Is this it?" Sage asked, picking up a sheet of yellow paper from the oak dining table.

"Yes!" Nina smiled. "What would I do without you?"

"I'm sure you'd do just fine," Sage said with conviction. "You're one of the most able people I know."

"I suppose you're right," Nina admitted, "but I sure enjoy having you around."

"I enjoy being around," Sage gave Nina a quick hug. "Now let's get going before it gets any hotter. The weatherman predicted a high of 101 today!"

"Oh my!" Nina declared. "I'm wilting just thinking about it." She followed Sage to her car, and they drove the few blocks to the town's only grocery store.

After finding everything on Nina's list, and a few things Sage needed, they chose a few items for their lunch.

"Let's take your groceries home, then have lunch at my house so you can see how the garden is doing?" Sage suggested.

"Oh, lets!" Nina agreed. "I love the summer flowers. They're so bold and bright. Are the coneflowers blooming? Do you have snapdragons this year?"

"Yes and yes," Sage laughed. "You'll see for yourself in a few minutes." The two women quickly put away Nina's groceries and were headed to Sage's house in a short time with their lunch fixings.

"I'm starving," Sage announced as they walked in to the coolness of her home. "Let's get that food ready!"

"It's only eleven," Nina reported, looking at her watch.

"I know," Sage replied, "but I didn't eat any breakfast. I hate to admit it, but I kinda overslept."

"Well, not everyone likes to get up with the roosters," Nina teased.

In the little kitchen, they unpacked the grocery bags.

"If you'll start on the fruit salad," Sage directed. "I'll put the sandwiches together." Nina removed plump red grapes and sweet-smelling cantaloupe from a white plastic grocery bag. "Here's a bowl and the melon ball scoop," Sage handed her the equipment, then took out a plastic cutting board. She opened a loaf of fresh focaccia from the store's bakery and sliced it crosswise on the board then spread on homemade basil pesto and began layering the smoked turkey, ham, farmer's cheese and red-leaf lettuce they'd purchased that morning.

"So," Nina began. "Are you getting pretty serious with Cade?"

"I'm not sure," Sage spoke hesitantly. "I like him a lot, but I feel unsure about a lot of things too."

"I guess that's normal," Nina commented. "I remember when I first dated your grandpa. I was definitely smitten, but it took a while before I felt sure about making a life-long commitment to him. That's a big step, and I know too many people who made a bad choice and then just lived with it. Luckily that didn't happen to me. Your Grandpa was a good man, and I never regretted marrying him." Nina laughed, a faraway look in her eyes. "That's not to say we never had a fight, but the making up was always worth it!" Sage grinned at the mischievous look on Nina's face.

"Grandpa was a good man. You were lucky."

"That I was," Nina readily agreed. She leaned over and gave Sage a quick hug. "You'll make the right choice," she reassured Sage. "I have faith in you."

"I wish I had it in myself." Sage chuckled, but a worried look remained in her eyes.

"Trust your intuition," Nina encouraged. "Most of the bad decisions I've made happened when I didn't listen to that little inner voice."

"I'm sure that's good advice," Sage agreed. "I'll work on it."

The women fixed their plates and carried them out to the little table in the yard. Sage pulled it a few feet to where it was shaded by a big cottonwood tree, and they sat down to eat.

"How's the book coming?" Nina inquired.

"Pretty good," Sage was glad to report. "I have a first draft nearly done, but it'll still take some revision." Sage picked up a slice of sandwich from her plate and took a bite. "Mmmm! I love sandwiches!" She mumbled, covering her mouth with her hand. She chewed slowly, and then continued. "I sent an excerpt from the book to some publishers and agents. I emailed one of my college professors, and she recommended that I go ahead and try to market it. I wasn't sure if I should wait until it was completely done, or go ahead. She said the whole process takes quite a while, and I should go ahead."

"How did you know who to send it to?" Nina wondered.

"I found a couple of books about how to get your work published," Sage continued. "I just followed what they said. Plus," she went on, "I went to the library and looked at who the publishers were for some other novels similar to mine. I targeted those."

"Sounds like you have it all planned and under control," Nina told her. "I knew you would!"

Laughing, Sage replied, "I'm glad you have enough confidence for both of us!"

They continued eating while discussing the garden and talking about what was blooming, what would be in bloom soon, and what work needed to be done. Sage told her grandmother about an idea she'd been tossing around for a small shade garden in the back part of the yard. Nina thought it a wonderful idea, and they discussed the specifics as they finished eating. After her last bite, Nina leaned back in her chair and yawned.

"I think you'd better take this old lady home for a nap," she said. "I still don't have all my strength back."

"It takes time," Sage reassured her. Picking up the dishes, Sage followed Nina into the house. She deposited the plates, glasses and silverware in the sink. "I'll run you home, then come back and wash these few things up."

"I'm too tired to argue," was Nina's reply.

CHAPTER TWENTY-ONE

"I gave Lloyd my notice today," Cade announced as they sat in his living room that night. The television cast an electronic glow across the room. Sage was silent for a moment.

"How long?" she finally asked.

"Two weeks," he told her. "Maybe longer if he can't find a replacement, but I really don't think he'll have too much trouble."

"He's going to miss you," she said. "He told me you're the best help he's had in a long time."

"Really?" Cade was surprised. "Well, that's nice to know."

"So what about us?" Sage asked.

"I don't want to lose you," Cade confessed. "I know that. Beyond that, I'm not sure." Pulling her close to him on the couch, he continued. "What do you want?"

"I don't want to lose you," she admitted. "But what does that mean? Canyon Ridge is quite a ways from here."

"Yes," he agreed. "A long-distance relationship wouldn't be easy. I suppose it could work for a while, maybe until we both figure out for sure what we want." Sage snuggled against him and he softly kissed the top of her head. "Would you ever be willing to live there? I mean, with me?" His question was tentative.

"I'm not sure. Maybe." Sage was honest. "I've thought about it," She admitted. "Do you mean just live together, or get married?" She hesitated to ask, not wanting it to sound like she was fishing for a proposal, but it mattered to her. She didn't believe in living together. If you loved someone enough to be with them, you loved them enough to marry them.

"The way I feel about you, I'd like us to be married." Cade looked at her intently. "I love you, Sage."

Tears filled her eyes. "I love you, too" she whispered.

"You're not supposed to cry when I say that," he teased her. "It's supposed to make you happy."

"It does," Sage laughed through her tears. "It's just scary too. Feeling so much for someone frightens me. Doesn't it you?"

"A lot," he admitted. "But it feels good, too. I feel like I've been waiting all my life to meet you."

She turned to him and pulled his mouth to hers, melting her lips against his and savoring the taste of him. It was a taste that never failed to cause a quickening in her belly. She moaned softly, and then pulled back. She knew how easily they could get lost in one another physically, and there was more to talk about. Looking at him, she continued.

"For the past couple of years, this place has been so perfect for me. I love it here, my house, being near Grandma; and running the café is perfect to supplement my writing income.

To be honest, the idea of leaving is kind of scary to me. It's like giving up my security.

"Ironic isn't it?" Cade sighed. "Inheriting this ranch is giving me a chance for the only security I've had in years."

"Why does life have to be so confusing?" Sage asked to no one in particular. She knew there was no answer to the question.

"I wonder that myself," Cade admitted. "I used to think some of us had hard lives because we deserved it; like we weren't worthy of having it easy, or if we finally earned it, then we would have a good life."

"That's crazy!" Sage admonished him.

"I know that now," he confessed. "but it took me a while to figure it out. The really scary thing is how quickly our fortunes can change. Just like me inheriting this ranch. I never in a million years would have dreamed it was possible. I figured if I worked really hard, and had some good luck, then maybe, someday, I'd be able to buy a small place. It's beyond my wildest dreams that one would be left to me."

"Yeah," Sage agreed. "I know what you mean. I think for me, it'd be like getting a book published, and having it hit the best-seller list. I picture myself spending most of my life writing, and maybe, if I'm lucky, getting a couple things published; but really hitting it big? I can hardly imagine that."

Cade gave her a squeeze. "This isn't solving our problem," he said softly.

"No," she whispered. "I guess if neither of us wants to lose the other, then we'll figure out something. It's a good place to start from. Grandma always told me, 'there's nothing that can't be solved if you want it bad enough!'"

"I think she's right," Cade agreed. "And we want each other pretty badly." His hand slid down to cup her breast, and he showed her just how much he wanted her.

*   *   *   *

The next week passed quickly. Sage worked on her book, sent off more queries to agents and publishers, and did some deep cleaning at the café. She always did that in the summer, because the week off between livestock sales gave her a chance to get those extras done. She washed all the windows, inside and out; cleaned out the cupboards, wiped out the fridge; and deep-cleaned the carpet even though she knew the latter was a somewhat useless activity. She liked the way her little café sparkled and smelled good, at least until the next sale when dirty boots tracked in again.

Cade spent his week working long hours. Lloyd seemed to want to get as much out of him as possible before he left. The older man had confessed he was worried about finding another hired man. Consequently, he and Buck put in a lot of miles traversing pastures whose grass was beginning to turn brown in the late summer heat. For the most part, Lloyd's cattle were healthy and his fences in good repair. He did have to doctor a Hereford cow for foot rot late one afternoon, but when he checked her a couple days later she was much improved. After the thorough job Cade had done with the cattle, he knew Lloyd could get by for a couple weeks without help if need be.

In the little time he had off, Cade went to the grocery store and procured boxes, then packed up his few belongings. His place was a mess, with open boxes piled around the rooms to allow access to those things he might still need. He'd spoken to Ruth Jamison again. The paperwork for the ranch transfer had all gone through. It was now officially his. A bubble of excitement filled him constantly now. He felt like a kid again. He couldn't wait to get to his place and start working on it; get it back in shape and running the way it had been when Sam had been alive.

Sage and Cade saw each other several nights that week, once going out for a burger at the local drive-in, other times cooking together at his place or hers. They didn't talk much about their situation, but their lovemaking took on an intensity and desperation that they both recognized. Neither could imagine the other not being there, not spending their evenings together, not sleeping in each other's arms. They realized phone calls would be small consolation after being accustomed to the real thing. Still, both seemed hesitant to discuss a deeper commitment. The timing just wasn't right. They'd only known one another a couple of months. Was that long enough on which to base a decision that could last a lifetime?

CHAPTER TWENTY-TWO

A week later, Cade was gone. Lloyd was in the process of interviewing replacements, and Sage was working frantically in an effort to fill the huge emptiness in her days. As she prepared for the first sale since Cade had gone, she watched a handful of men file one by one in to Lloyd's office to be interviewed.

She worked quietly in the café, tearing up an assortment of greens and slicing crisp cucumbers and fresh, garden tomatoes for the dinner salad. She then scrubbed and peeled ten pounds of russet potatoes, cubed them, and covered them with water before setting them in the refrigerator to be cooked the following morning. As the day wound down, she found herself looking for things to do so she wouldn't have to go home to an empty house; a house whose solitude she'd previously enjoyed but that now seemed to be only empty and lonely.

Finally, when she could think of nothing else that could be done at the café, Sage drove home. After pulling up in front of her house, she sat there with the engine idling as she stared around her yard. Late summer flowers filled the space with color and texture. Ornamental grasses dotted the beds, interspersed with sassy, black-eyed susans and double, pink petunias. Trumpet-shaped four-o-clocks waved their pink and white and yellow petals, enticing hummingbird moths to their sweet nectar. Sage loved all the seasons in her garden, but spring and summer were the best. Somehow, the variety and profusion of blooms, the varied shades of foliage, the elusive fragrances of those seasons, all served to highlight her garden at its best. After staring vacantly for several minutes, Sage's rumbling stomach brought her back to the present. Thinking quickly through what her cupboards held, she decided that a trip to the local pizzeria was in order. It was either that or the grocery store for something to cook, and she didn't feel like waiting that long to eat.

Since the Pizza Palace was only three blocks from her house, Sage turned off the car's ignition and set out on foot, hoping the exercise might help her sleep. The nights since Cade left had been long and her sleep restless. Strolling along the quiet streets, she thought back to the morning Cade had moved. She'd helped him load his boxes and furniture, as had Lloyd and two other guys who worked at the sale barn. It had only taken a couple of hours. He didn't have much. The last item had been to hook up his beat-up green two-horse trailer to the pickup and load Buck. Sage watched as Cade slid his saddle, horse blanket and bridle, along with two bags of feed and a bale of prairie hay into the trailer stall opposite Buck.

Finally, when there was nothing left to load, he turned to Sage.

"Well, I guess it's time to get on the road." She could see the longing in those brown eyes already. It brought tears to her eyes, and she blinked them back furiously, determined not to cry.

"I guess it is," she whispered. A stray tear slid down her cheek, and she hurriedly brushed it away. Cade pulled her to him.

"Baby, it'll be okay," his voice was muffled, his mouth pressed against her head. "I'll call as soon as I get a phone hooked up. Hopefully by tomorrow," he promised.

"Okay," she agreed, "and I'll come up next weekend."

"It's gonna be a long week without you, honey." Cade kissed her softly, trying to memorize how her mouth felt on his.

"Same here," she replied, her arms squeezing him tightly.

It had taken three days for Cade to get his phone hooked up, by which time Sage had gotten worried. She imagined him lying in the ditch, his crumpled truck overturned beside him; she pictured him asleep in a hospital bed, tubes and monitors attached to his body; but he finally called, and her worries had been without merit. He apologized for the delay, and explained that the phone company had been extra busy due to a thunderstorm that had knocked out service to a number of phones in the area. Sage breathed a sigh of relief, and then proceeded to fire questions at him about the happenings at the ranch. He answered as many as he could, then laughed, interrupting her to ask what she had been up to.

"I can't keep up with all your questions, baby," he said. "I can't wait for you to get here and see what I've done. The place looks so much better already. You won't believe it!"

"Only two more days," Sage reminded him. "And I haven't been doing anything exciting," she continued. "The sale is over, and I'm already planning for next week. I did some yard work last night, just mowing and deadheading."

"Deadheading?" Cade laughed. "That sounds violent!"

Sage laughed, "it means pinching off the spent blossoms so more new ones will open."

Their conversation continued for nearly an hour, until Cade admitted that he was exhausted and begged off to get to bed.

"Call me tomorrow night," he told Sage. "I'm going to work on cleaning up the house tomorrow, so I'll have more to report. I was thinking that maybe when you're here we could go to town and look for some new furniture?"

"I'd love that!" Excitement tinged her voice, and Cade smiled.

"I thought you would," he chuckled. "You're such a female!"

"Lucky for you that I am," Sage admonished happily. "Otherwise, our relationship would be very different!"

"That's true," he admitted.

"Well, you get to bed now," Sage encouraged him. "I know you must be exhausted."

"Weary to the bone," he declared. "'night, baby"

"Goodnight, Cade."

The next morning Sage bustled around her house. By ten a.m., she had laundry going, a loaf of wheat bread in the oven, and sprinklers dousing her flowerbeds with a much needed drink. She wanted to get an early start the next morning on her trip to see Cade. A little while later, she lay back on her sofa inhaling the nutty aroma of the bread baking, as she took a much needed break from her preparations.

Just as she relaxed, her breathing deep and even, her mind cleared of her to-do list, the deep, tonal ring of her phone interrupted. She almost didn't answer because she was pretty sure it wasn't Cade, and she couldn't think of anyone else she wanted to talk with at the moment. Ultimately, her curiosity got the better of her, and she rushed to pick up before voice mail beat her to it.

"Hello?" She struggled to breath evenly after her mad dash to the phone.

"Hello," a distant sounding voice replied. "Is this Sage Claremont?"

"Yes, it is," she responded. "What can I do for you?"

"This is Rhonda Gaskill. I'm an agent with Heart Publishing."

"Oh," Sage's heart missed a beat.

"I have a copy of the manuscript you're working on here in front of me, and I have to tell you, it's marvelous!"

"Well, good," Sage felt tongue-tied.

"I read your story yesterday, after one of our junior editors recommended it. I have to say, your plot is creative and I'm impressed by your writing style."

"Thanks," Sage replied.

"So, you must be wondering why I'm calling?" the woman asked.

"Yes," Sage said. "I'm definitely curious!"

Rhonda Gaskill chuckled. "I'll tell you then," she continued. "We're interested in working with you on this piece. We think that, with a few revisions, it could definitely be publishable."

"Really?" Surprise filled Sage's voice.

"Yes, really." The other woman responded. "How long have you been writing Ms. Claremont?"

"I finished my creative writing degree two years ago," Sage explained. "And I've had a couple of articles published, but this is my first novel."

"Wow," Ms. Gaskill went on. "Now I'm even more impressed. This is quite a piece of writing for a first novel."

"Again, thanks," Sage replied.

"Anyway, Sage. May I call you Sage?"

"Of course."

"And you must call me Rhonda," the woman requested. "I think we'll be working closely. At least I hope so."

"What do you have in mind?" Sage asked, finally getting her thoughts together.

"What we'd like," Ms. Gaskill described, "is for you to come to New York for a week, as our guest of course, and work with myself and another editor on revising your manuscript. I'd like to mail you a contract that outlines in detail what we are offering. Then, when you have a chance to look it over, you can call me."

"Sounds perfect!" Sage replied. Then, not wanting to sound overly excited, she continued. "I'll look forward to reviewing the contract."

"Great," the other woman replied. "And I hope we will be working together in the near future!"

"Thanks," Sage replied, "and I'll be watching for that contract."

After hanging up, Sage let out a whoop! She jumped up and down, yelling, then raced to the phone and dialed Grandma Nina's number.

"You're never going to believe this!" She announced excitedly as soon as Nina said hello.

"Believe what?" the older woman smiled at the sound of her granddaughter's voice.

"I just got a call from a publisher in New York! They like my book!"

"Really?" Nina's voice rose an octave. "What did they say?"

"It was a woman named Rhonda Gaskill from Heart Publishing," Sage related. "She had my manuscript that I'd submitted, and she likes it. She wants to work with me on some revisions. They really think my work is publishable!"

"Honey, that's wonderful!" Nina announced. "I know you're an excellent writer, and now others are recognizing it too! I knew it was only a matter of time."

"Thanks Grandma," Sage accepted the compliment, "but you're not exactly unbiased," she said wryly.

"That's true," Nina admitted. "But I know good writing when I see it. Have you called your parents yet?" She enquired.

"No. You're the first person I've told."

"Then you'd better hang up and call them right now!" Nina encouraged. "I can't wait to hear what they think."

"I'll call them now," Sage said.

"Wait," Nina interrupted. "I think this calls for a celebratory dinner. How about you pick me up tonight about seven and I'll take you out?"

"Sounds awesome!" Sage accepted, and the two hung up so she could call her parents.

Throughout the rest of the day, Sage floated through her trip preparations on a cloud of excitement. She couldn't wait to get to Canyon Ridge to tell Cade her big news. She wanted to tell him in person so she could see the excitement in his face. She dashed to the mailbox as soon as she saw the mailman approaching, even though she knew it was too soon to expect anything from the publisher. She finished her laundry, packed a few clothes, and watered her flowers deeply to get them through the weekend. Her gardens were filled with the blossoms of late summer. Blankets of purple petunias threatened to overtake a clump of snapdragon's bright yellow spikes, while the four-o'clock's trumpet-shaped pink blossoms added profusions of color to the evening show. Sage pulled a shiny, green garden hose around her yard, the cool blades of fescue tickling her bare feet. She loved being in her garden, being rewarded for the hours she spent there by the beauty of her surroundings. *I should spend more time enjoying this,* she thought, *instead of always working when I'm out here.* But she knew she loved the work as much as the aesthetics, and before she realized it, she had leaned over to pluck a weed from among the basil. She inhaled the savory scent of her herb garden, and plucked a few stems of parsley to add to a potato salad she planned to take to Cade's.

A little while later, while water from the hose soaked the roots of a large sedum, Sage glanced at her watch and realized she had about five minutes to get ready for her dinner with Nina. She scurried to shut off the water, and then rushed inside to change. Nina was waiting near the parking lot when Sage pulled up. She climbed into the car and gave her granddaughter a big hug.

"I still can't believe it!" Nina gushed. "My favorite granddaughter is having a book published!"

"I'm your only granddaughter," Sage laughed. "AND I have to make revisions first, and then hope they still like it."

"Oh, they'll like it," Nina reassured her. "Like I always told you, 'believe in yourself.'"

"I remember," Sage said, patting her grandma's hand. "Not a day goes by that I don't remember it."

CHAPTER TWENTY-THREE

The next morning, Sage got up early, loaded her car, and was on the road by 8:00 a.m. She enjoyed driving through the broad rolling hills, and appreciated the fact that they were still a bit green even in late summer. The area had been blessed with several nice rains in the past month. The drive went quickly and before she knew it Sage was pulling into Canyon Ridge. She was impressed with the residential part of town, but thought the downtown area wasn't as nice as the business district in Hope. Several blocks into town, she saw the Horseshoe Diner on her left, and pulled into the parking lot. Taking her cell phone from her purse, she dialed Cade's number.

"Hey Sexy!" she said when he picked up.

"You're the sexy one," he chuckled. "Are you here?"

"I'm here," she confirmed. "Come meet me. I can't wait to see you!" They had agreed that he would drive to town and meet her, and then she would follow him to the ranch. He'd tried giving her directions, but after she heard him describe the winding road and multiple turns, she begged off and asked him to meet her.

"It'll take me about 20 minutes to get there," Cade explained. "Go on in the Horseshoe and get something to drink."

"Sounds good," she agreed. "I bought a diet soda a little while back, and I definitely need to use their facilities!"

Cade laughed. "I'll see you soon, baby."

"Can't wait," she sighed and hung up. Grabbing her purse, she headed into the café to wait.

An hour later, after a quick lunch, Sage found herself encased in a cloud of dust following Cade's truck as they headed for the ranch. She slowed down a bit and let him get far enough ahead so she could see her surroundings. The country was more hilly than what she was used to. The canyons were steeper and here and there scrub pines dotted the landscape. When he finally turned off onto a long, winding driveway, Sage looked ahead excitedly. She couldn't wait to glimpse of his ranch again , and she wasn't disappointed.

Rounding a curve, the white ranch house and red outbuildings came into view. She was once again taken aback by the idyllic scene before her. Pulling up next to Cade's truck in front of the house, Sage climbed from her car.

"Cade! This place is so awesome! I can't get over how beautiful it is!" She grabbed him in a big hug.

"I think so," he hugged her back, the pride evident in his voice, "come on and I'll show you what I've done." He took her hand and pulled her toward the barn.

They toured the barn, looked at the old tractor and truck, the chicken house, and another little shed. Cade told her that Sam had used it to raise a couple of pigs each year. Peering over the low wooden fence, she saw a metal trough and an old, rusty tank.

"Let's look at the house now," she pulled him in that direction. "I can't wait to see all the things you've done!"

"I'm glad you saw it before," he walked beside her, watching her face, "you can really appreciate how much better it looks."

"I'll definitely appreciate it," she laughed. "You've worked so hard all week!"

"Cade opened the back door, then stepped back and let Sage walk in first. The old kitchen gleamed from Cade's thorough cleaning. It needed a lot of updating, but Sage could see tremendous potential. The room was large and open. Windows over the sink and near the table provided a wide vista of the hay meadow in front and the big back yard. The old Formica countertops were worn, and the linoleum floor chipped, but the pine cabinets, with some elbow grease, looked promising.

"This is great!" She exclaimed. "It's huge!"

"Yes," Cade agreed. "It was Carol's favorite room. She loved to cook, and when company came over everyone gathered in the kitchen."

"Okay, proceed with the tour," she directed, gently pushing him toward the living room door.

"I'm going," he laughed, grabbing her hand again. Sage was even more impressed with the rest of the house than she had been on her first visit. The rooms were all large and open, with windows that showed the gorgeous countryside. The carpets were outdated, and Cade had taken down most of the curtains. He described how some of them had hung in shreds, having disintegrated with age.

Sage laughed when he showed her the bathroom. Its pink tiled walls and deep, pink tub reminded her of her grandparent's bathroom on the ranch. Grandma Nina had chosen the color scheme herself, and had been so proud of her modern bathroom.

"This looks just like my grandparent's bathroom on their ranch," she described to him Nina's pride in the room. "It was the first room they remodeled when they finally had enough money to fix up the house. Grandma fancied herself quite the interior designer!"

"I'm sure she did," Cade chuckled as he leaned down and began nuzzling Sage's neck. A tingle ran up her spine, as every nerve ending in her body sprang to attention.

"You're distracting me from the tour," Sage teasingly admonished him.

"Tour?" He feigned confusion. "Oh yes," he paused between nibbles along her collarbone. "Now I remember. Have I showed you my bedroom?"

Sage giggled. "Yes, you did, but I haven't seen your new sheets yet. It's important for me to understand what colors you like for when I help you select your new furniture."

"I agree totally," he murmured. His hands slid up from her waist and cupped her full breasts. She could feel his arousal pressed against her bottom. Turning to face him, she slid her arms around his neck and pulled his mouth toward hers as he backed from the room.

"Lead the way, cowboy."

Over dinner that night, Sage told him about her call from the editor in New York. Her eyes sparkled with excitement, and Cade couldn't help smiling.

"This is a dream come true for you, isn't it baby?" He said, putting his hand over hers on the table.

"Completely!" She agreed. "It's what I've been working for ever since I finished college."

"I'm proud of you," he said.

"Thanks," she smiled. "I'm proud of you too. This place is wonderful, and you've done so much here already. It's like everything is happening for both of us, isn't it?"

"Yes," he agreed. "and the best part is, we met each other. Without you, Sage, this place wouldn't mean so much to me. Without you to share it with, I mean."

"That's how I feel too," she admitted. "I couldn't wait to get here and share my news with you in person. I almost called to tell you," she described, "but I wanted to see your face."

"So what does it all mean?" Cade questioned. "The contract and editor and all that?"

"I'm not sure yet," she told him. "I'll know more after I get the contract." She recited her conversation with Rhonda Gaskill, filling in with the little she knew about the publishing industry.

"So you'll have to go to New York?" Cade asked.

"Yes, it sounds that way, at least for a little while."

"How long?" he wondered.

"I'm not sure," she admitted. "I suppose it depends on the extent of the revisions. Rhonda only mentioned a week or so."

"I hope it isn't for too long."

"Me too," she agreed. "But I'll stay however long I need to. However long it takes to get my book ready to publish."

"What about the café?"

"I've been thinking about that. I'll probably ask Ellie if she'll manage it for a few weeks. She'd be my first choice anyway, and I think she'll say yes."

"Good plan," Cade replied.

The weekend passed quickly, too quickly for both Cade and Sage. On Saturday afternoon, they drove into town and went to the local furniture stores. They were able to find a sofa and two recliners that they both liked, and Sage found a perfect oak coffee table at a little antique store. Afterward, they went to a big discount store and stocked up on dishes, cookware, and utensils, then finished their shopping spree with a stop at the grocery store. By the time they got back to the ranch, they were both exhausted. Cade pulled two old lawn chairs from the garage and hosed the dust from them, and they sat on the porch with glasses of iced tea, waiting for the furniture delivery truck to arrive.

"I wish you weren't going back," Cade sighed. "It feels so right to have you here."

"It feels right to be here," Sage admitted. "But what does that mean for us?"

"That's what we need to figure out," Cade replied.

"I know you're right," she agreed. "But right now I have to focus on getting this book deal going." She saw disappointment flicker across his face before he could hide it. "You're very important to me, Cade," she reached across and covered his hand with her. "But so is this. This deal could make or break my writing career. I have to give it everything I've got." She gave his hand a squeeze. "I can't give you everything you deserve in our relationship if I feel that I've sacrificed my dreams in the process."

"You're right, of course." He looked at her. "I would never ask you to give up your dreams. I just hate the idea of not being with you, not seeing you for weeks at a time."

"I hate that too," she confessed. "We'll just have to call every day. I want to know everything you do here, every detail. And I'll tell you how my writing goes, and what the publisher says. Deal?"

"Deal," he said, pulling her toward him for a kiss.

CHAPTER TWENTY-FOUR

A couple of days after Sage returned home, the package from the publisher arrived. She took it immediately to Grandma Nina's, and the two women poured over the contract, reading the fine print carefully. Steaming mugs of coffee sat cooling, and untouched, by each of them.

"What are first rights?" Nina wondered.

"What about these percentages?" Sage queried. "Do they look fair? How am I supposed to know?"

"Good question," Nina responded. "I suppose this is why you should have an agent."

"I think you're right," Sage grinned, "and I know just the person to help me find one." Taking her blue leather wallet from her purse, she pulled a yellow square of paper out, and picked up her cell phone.

"Who?" Nina eyes flashed with curiosity.

"My professor and mentor, Dr. Livingston. She taught some of my creative writing classes, and she has had a number of her works published." Nina smiled supportively, and went to warm the coffee while Sage waited for her call to go through.

"Pam Livingston," Sage heard the familiar voice answer on the other end of the line.

"Dr. Livingston? It's Sage Claremont."

"Sage! How are you?" Dr. Livingston's warm tone reminded Sage of their talks in the coziness of the professor's office. The two had spend many sessions discussing Sage's writing, Pam's writing, and work by other author's that both women enjoyed.

"Great!" Sage said. "And you? How are things in the English Department?"

"I'm fine, and the English Department forges onward as usual! It's so good to hear from you, Sage."

"I've been going to call for ages," Sage admitted. "I have some exciting news!"

"Well," Pam encouraged. "Don't keep me in suspense!"

"I have a publisher interested in my book!"

"Congratulations! That's awesome!" Pam gushed. "Tell me the details!"

Sage related the phone call and then told her mentor about the contract.

"Is this the book you were planning when you left here?" Pam enquired.

"Yeah, but it took me a while to get going on it." Sage gave a brief timeline of her writing process. "It's a bit different from what I first thought I'd write, but you know how that always happens?"

"I sure do. Nothing I write ever turns out to be what I thought it would," Pam agreed.

"I need some advice," Sage finally admitted.

"Shoot," Pam waited to hear Sage's question.

"I need to know if the percentages and other details of the contract are okay," Sage began. She went on to describe the specifics, and then listened carefully while Dr. Livingston gave her some suggestions.

"Overall, it sounds pretty good," Pam directed. "Ask them about the few things I mentioned, and if they agree to change those, then I'd say go for it! Oh yes, and keep me posted."

"You know I will," Sage smiled at her Grandmother, who was waiting impatiently to hear all the details.

"Thanks Pam. You're a lifesaver!"

"Well, I do what I can," Pam could hear Sage's excitement barely contained in her voice. "Get those publisher people on the phone and get this worked out, then call me from New York!"

"Okay, and thanks again!" After hanging up, Sage related the gist of the conversation to Nina. The two spent another hour pouring over the contract, taking notes, and writing down questions. Finally, Sage called Rhonda Gaskill's office, only to learn that Rhonda was out for the rest of the afternoon. Sage left her name and number and then hung up, feeling somewhat deflated. She had been so pumped to get this all taken care of, and now it would have to wait another day.

Seeing the disappointment in her granddaughter's face, Nina suggested they go back to Sage's house and get some yard work done, then cook dinner on the grill and eat outside to enjoy the fruits of their labor. Sage forced a smile and agreed. Lying in her bed that night, she realized that Nina's suggestion had been a good one. Gardening had relieved some of her tension and helped the time pass, and when dinner was over and she took her grandmother home, Sage thought again how much she appreciated her friendship with the older woman.

191

*　　　　*　　　　*　　　　*
*　　　　*

     Looking out the window of the Northwest Airlines 727, Sage watched the heartland pass beneath her. She thought of the people like herself, like the men and women who ate in her café each week, who lived in the little farming and ranching communities that dotted the landscape rushing beneath her. She knew many of them had never been to New York City. She also knew that many of them had no desire to see the Big Apple. They were content in their safe little towns, in their clean air, their wide-open spaces, and their circle of friends who were more like family. Sage could understand how they felt, but she also knew her own need for the city, the culture and restaurants and museums, the crowds and energy that only a large city could offer. Her heart beat rapidly as her mind raced thinking about her upcoming days working with Rhonda and others at Heart Publishing. They'd faxed her a schedule and itinerary, and she had looked on the internet to see what the Heart Publishing building looked like. The pictures she had seen ran through her mind like trailers from a movie she couldn't wait to see, and she shifted in her seat, restless and unable to focus on the book she'd brought.

     The hours passed. It wasn't a terribly long flight, only about 2 and a half hours, and Sage was finally able to settle down and read. An elderly woman sat next to her, and they talked a bit. The woman, who introduced herself as Gladys Johnson, described her recent visit to see her new great-granddaughter in Greeley, Co. Sage politely oohed and aahed over the pictures, and Gladys beamed, her blue eyes sparkling in her lined face. Sage speculated that this is exactly what Nina would act like when finally presented with a great-grandchild.

     "We'll begin our descent into New York's La Guardia airport in about five minutes," the pilot announced. "Please fasten your safety belts and return your trays to the upright position." Butterflies well up in Sage's stomach as she snapped her lap belt into place and pulled it snug.

"Well, we're almost there," excitement filled Gladys' voice as she peered out the window. Sage smiled at the older woman's barely contained enthusiasm. Her own excitement was held in check by a healthy dose of nervousness. She wiped her sweaty palms on her denim-encased thighs. A black leather jacket over a crisp, white blouse completed her travel attire. Sage stretched her long legs as much as she was able to, thankful to be in the aisle seat, which allowed her more leg room. She noticed a distinguished looking man in the seat across from her looking at her outstretched leg and black leather boots with appreciation. She smiled when she caught his eye, acknowledging his interest, and then looked away. He had nothing on Cade, she thought, recalling her lover's toned and muscular physique, his dreamy brown eyes, and well, other parts she didn't dare start thinking about!

Feeling the plane begin to descend, Sage leaned her head back against the seat and closed her eyes. Taking a deep breath, she imagined the next few hours; collecting her luggage, finding a cab, riding through the city, and finally, arriving at the apartment where she would be staying during her time in the Big Apple. Rhonda Gaskill, the editor Sage had spoken with from Heart Publishing, told Sage that the company kept a small apartment for their clients who were there for an extended stay. It was on the Upper East Side of Manhattan only a few blocks from Heart Publishing.

Exiting the plane, Sage's excitement grew. Her dream was unfolding! Here I am in New York City, and tomorrow I'll be meeting with an editor to work on my book, she thought! She strode confidently through the crowds at La Guardia, easily finding her luggage terminal and picking up her dark floral

Pullman suitcase. Slinging her backpack over her shoulder, she pulled the handle up on her suitcase and headed for the exit.

Once outside, Sage caught the eye of a cab driver wearing a red turban, his swarthy features making her think of an Arab sheik. Your imagination's working overtime, Sage, she told herself as she approached the yellow taxi. Giving the driver her address, Sage handed over her luggage, and then watched as he loaded it into the trunk. Sliding into the rear seat, she sat back and watched the metropolitan landscape unfold. Traffic and people were everywhere, traveling with a purpose that matched Sage's own. She felt invigorated by the hustle and bustle, and watched excitedly out the cab window, looking for landmarks and taking in the multicultural atmosphere.

In less time than she thought possible, the yellow cab pulled up in front of a stately brown brick building. A green canvas awning reached to the curb, and Sage exited the cab under its cover. The cabbie unloaded her bag, and she paid him with crisp bills she'd gotten from the Hope bank the day before. The cost, while not a surprise, left Sage thinking how glad she was that she didn't have to take a cab very often! Her small income from the café wouldn't go far in this city. Grabbing the handle of her bag, she walked up to the building. The doorman was expecting her, and pointed her in the direction of apartment 3C. The small apartment welcomed her despite its starkly modern décor. It was so different from her own Victorian-style house, but she found herself soothed by the clean lines and simplicity of the space.

Sinking down on the sofa, she sighed and let relief wash over her. She'd been nervous about the trip, and it felt good just to be here. She pulled off her boots and reached for the remote, then skimmed through the channels until she found local news and weather. A vibrant dark-haired woman predicted a beautiful day for tomorrow, and Sage thought how the weather matched her mood. Her rumbling stomach reminded her that she hadn't had a real meal all day, and she reached for a phone book laying on a table near the sofa. As she was skimming through the restaurant section looking for pizza delivery, the phone rang.

"Hello," Sage started.

"Is this Sage?" A familiar voice asked.

"Rhonda?" Sage asked.

"Yes," Rhonda Gaskill sounded relieved and excited at the same time. "I see you made it to our fair city."

"I did," Sage relayed. "I've only been here a little while. I was just relaxing a bit. By the way, this apartment is great!"

"Glad you like it," Rhonda replied. "It'll be comfortable and convenient for you. So what are your plans for tonight?" Rhonda continued. "Do you have any questions for me before I head home?"

"Well, the first one that comes to mind is could you tell me a good place for take-out pizza?" Rhonda laughed, and gave Sage the number of her favorite nearby pizzeria. "I think, that after some food, I'll be ready for a hot bath and bed." Sage laughed. "And I have the directions to your office for tomorrow morning. I think I'm all set."

"Great!" Rhonda answered. "See you in the morning then.

Sage leaned back on the sofa, imagining her first day with an editor working on her book.

*   *   *   *
*

Later that evening, after a delicious white pizza and a hot bubble bath, Sage lay on the queen size bed luxuriating in the softness of the white sheets and the fluffy comforter. Using her cell phone, she dialed Cade's number and waited impatiently for his deep voice to answer.

"Hello?" Cade sounded out of breath when he answered after about five rings.

"Hey gorgeous, you sound all husky and out of breath. Makes me think of naughty things!" She chuckled.

"I was in the shower," he laughed, "now I'm standing here naked and dripping."

"Mmm! Now that definitely gives me naughty ideas!"

"Thinking about your ideas is causing a reaction," Cade admitted.

"Maybe you should dry off, lover," Sage suggested huskily, " and then we can talk more about your 'reaction'."

"Now that's the best idea I've heard all day." Arousal filled his voice. How about I call you back in five minutes or so?"

"I'll be waiting," Sage whispered, her fingers lightly caressing her naked breast.

CHAPTER TWENTY-FIVE

Sage woke early and laid in the darkened room letting the sounds of the city fill her senses. Even at this time of morning, traffic noise and an occasional horn honking drifted through the walls. Being accustomed to the quietness of small-town Hope, Sage's senses were attuned to the noise of people's lives going on around her. Excitement filled her as she speculated about her day ahead. Feeling almost giddy, she slid from between the sheets and strode to the bathroom. Turning on the taps, she watched as hot water fell like rain from the huge shower head, hitting the ceramic-tiled shower floor in a deluge. She'd always wanted a big shower head like this one, and she stepped under the downpour relishing the feeling of the hot water streaming down her body in delicious rivulets. She lathered her hair, rinsed the suds from her reddish-blonde curls, then worked in conditioner letting the rinse perform its magic while she soaped her body. After a relaxing rinse, she stepped out onto the fluffy bath mat and pulled a huge, soft towel from the rack and rubbed herself dry.

After donning a straight black skirt, a gray silk blouse, and low-heeled black boots, Sage walked to the kitchen and began looking through the cupboards. She discovered a small coffee pot, and set about brewing a pot, then searched the fridge for something to eat. Yogurt and an orange fit the bill, and Sage stood at the counter as she ate. Her mind was on the day ahead, and she barely tasted the food. Glancing at the clock, she realized it was time to head out. Grabbing a light, coral cardigan from her suitcase, Sage exited the apartment. Soon she was on the street and striding in the direction of Heart Publishing. The business of the city exhilarated her, and she felt as if she were on a special mission, a life-fulfilling journey.

*   *   *   *

A cool morning breeze carried the birds' songs into Cade's bedroom. They called to him, filling his dreams and singing him to wakefulness. He opened his eyes and stretched, the warm sheets sliding smoothly against his skin. He threw back his covers and stood, reaching his arms up high to stretch. Cade glanced out the window as morning's first rays pierced the darkness. He sauntered to the kitchen, comfortable with his nakedness, with his place in nature. Cade started a pot of coffee, then pulled a heavy, cast iron skillet from the cabinet and set it on the stove. After coating it with a drizzling of vegetable oil, he pulled a carton of eggs and package of sausage links from his refrigerator and began to cook his breakfast. His mind drifted to Sage, wondering what she was doing at that moment, half-way across the country. Was she thinking of him? Did she feel out of place in city? He thought of their conversation last night, and his cock swelled. Closing his eyes, he grasped his shaft and squeezed it, tugging lightly against the head as he remembered Sage's voice, the husky sound of her arousal, her moans when he asked her to touch herself. Sliding the skillet from the burner, Cade returned to his bed to relive the pleasure.

*   *   *   *   *

"Oh Cade," Sage gushed. "You can't believe how awesome my day was!" Cade couldn't help smiling into the receiver when he heard the excitement in her voice. He imagined her voice must have had the same tone on Christmas morning when she was a child. Being a woman made it that much more attractive.

"Tell me," he encouraged. "I want to hear everything!"

"It was beyond amazing!" she began. "Everyone there was so nice and so helpful, and they really like my book! That's the best part of all!" Cade chuckled, loving the confidence in her voice. She described her day, from what it was like to be in a wonderful city like New York, to the people who worked at Heart Publishing, to the fabulous deli sandwiches they'd eaten during their working lunch. "It's wonderful here, Cade," she went on. "The city itself is exhilarating! Everyone here seems to have an important purpose, a mission they must fulfill."

"It's the same here," Cade reminded her.

"Oh, I know," she admitted. "but it just seems different, like people have a greater sense of the importance of their work." Cade thought about what she described. He'd observed that people in rural areas were less vocal about their purpose. Many times, they were born to it, lived it without pomp or discussion. Nevertheless, it ran deeply in their veins.

They went about fulfilling their destiny in the shadow of a vast land, knowing that their mark was a tiny scratch on an ancient surface.

"Maybe city folks just talk more about it," he offered.

"Maybe," Sage replied, but her tone indicated that she didn't agree. Secretly, Sage was annoyed by Cade's lack of understanding about the feeling she was experiencing. "Well, anyway," she went on, "I'm having a great time here, and I love the city."

"Great," Cade tried to sound happy for her. "Well, I'd better get to bed. I have a busy day tomorrow."

"Okay," her voice was hesitant now, the wind gone from her sails. "So do I," she finished. After hanging up, she sat on the sofa, with the TV. playing silently to the quiet room. She wasn't sure what had happened, but she knew she didn't feel good about how their conversation had ended. Sage put on her pajamas, then went back to the television and flipped to her favorite cooking show, hoping to take her mind off Cade. Just as she was getting into a segment about preparing a beef roast with a dry herb rub, her phone rang. She grabbed it, and checked the caller i.d. only to find it was her grandmother calling. She tried not to feel disappointed, even though she very much hoped Cade would call back and apologize for putting the brakes on her excitement about the city.

"Hey Grandma!" Sage answered.

"Hello," Nina's familiar voice comforted Sage. "I had to call and see how your first day with the editors went?"

"It was awesome!" Sage began. "I had so much fun!" She proceeded to regale her grandmother with details about the day.

"I'm envious," Nina interjected. "I've always dreamed of the very things you describe."

"I know," Sage replied, "and I wish you were here."

"Me too," the older woman admitted. "You'll just have to tell me every detail." Her voice trailed off.

"You sound tired, grandma?" Sage enquired. "Are you feeling okay?"

"Oh, yes, I suppose I am." Nina tried to sound cheerful. "Just feeling a bit worn out. I'm sure it's nothing. Don't you worry about me," she finished.

"Maybe you should go see Dr. Rommel, just for a check-up." Sage suggested. "It can't hurt anything."

"I don't think that's necessary," Nina explained. "I'll just get to bed early tonight. There's nothing wrong with me that a good night's sleep won't cure."

"Well," Sage hesitated. "If you're sure."

"I'm sure, honey," Nina reassured her. "You just have fun with your book and don't worry about me."

"I'm glad you called, Grandma. If it wasn't for your encouragement, I wouldn't be here."

"I don't believe that for a second," Nina declared. "Now, I'm going to hang up and get to bed, and you should do the same."

"Bye, grandma," Sage closed her little phone and laid it on the end table. Leaning her head back against the sofa, she closed her eyes and relaxed. The TV played softly in the background. Several minutes later she decided Cade wasn't going to call, and she went to bed. Despite being upset with him, the busyness and excitement of her day had left her feeling exhausted, and she quickly fell asleep.

CHAPTER TWENTY-SIX

Sage's days followed a similar routine during the rest of the week. She started early each day working with her editor, going through the pages of her book, editing, revising, fleshing out certain parts with more details, and improving the realism of the dialogue. Sometimes the small group ordered lunch to be delivered to them, while other days they walked to small cafes nearby. Sage's exhilaration for the city and her infatuation with the whole process of publishing did not wane.

The night after her conversation with Cade, she waited impatiently for him to call, and when he didn't, she paced the floor debating with herself whether to call him, or just let him stew; if in fact he was stewing at all! Maybe he'd gone to town; maybe he was still outside working; maybe a nice neighbor girl had come over to welcome him! The more time she spent considering what Cade might be doing, the madder she became! How dare he not call her, not apologize for his attitude of the previous night! He knew how important this was to her, and there was no excuse for his behavior!

Morgandy Caye

At the peak of her indignation, Sage snatched up the phone and dialed Cade's number. Pacing and fuming, she listened to the ringing. After the tenth ring with no answer, she hung up, deflated. What if something happened to him, she wondered? Maybe he hadn't called because he was in the hospital? In a coma perhaps? Sage finally showered and got ready for bed, calling several more times in the interim, but still receiving no answer. Feeling decidedly weepy, she crawled into bed and shut out the light. Despite her doubt of ever falling asleep, Sage drifted off rather quickly. Her sleep was fitful, and she awoke feeling a bit tired and out-of-sorts. She vacillated between worry and anger when she thought of Cade, and tried calling once more before leaving for Heart Publishing and another day's work.

Several times throughout the day, Sage made mental notes to insist that Cade get an answering machine and a cell phone. She felt so frustrated not being able to get in touch with him. Despite her distractions, work progressed on her book. She felt most of the team's suggestions were good ones, and she could see how her story improved and her characters became more real as she implemented the changes.

Over dinner that night at a Manhattan pub, Rhonda Gaskill and Sage discussed the progress on the book. Both women were pleased with how it was coming along, and Rhonda felt that they could get through what was necessary by the end of the week. Then it would be Sage's job to take home the suggestions and implement them. As they talked, they both enjoyed Caesar salads topped with grilled chicken, and several mugs of cold beer brewed on sight.

After a while, the conversation veered away from work, and toward more personal topics. Rhonda told Sage about her recent divorce, and Sage described her relationship with Cade.

The women found in one another an understanding listener and good confidante.

Part way through the evening, a man approached their table.

"Rhonda Gaskill?" He asked.

"Yes," Rhonda responded. "Have we met?"

"Several years ago at a writing conference." He reminded her. "I was presenting a session on developing plot in a mystery novel. You sat in on my session. If I remember right, you presented right after me?"

"Oh yes!" Rhonda memory came back to her. "Roger isn't it?" She fished for his name. "I'm sorry, I don't remember your last name."

"It is Roger," he laughed. "And don't feel bad about forgetting my name. I confess that I asked the bartender what your name was!" Rhonda laughed.

"Cheater!" She teased him.

"I did remember your face," he insisted, as if that gave him the edge. "And the last name is Hayden."

"Roger Hayden. Yes," Rhonda reminisced. "Your session was very interesting. Are you still writing mysteries?"

"Sure am," he grinned. "My new one is due out next month. I'm in town finalizing it all."

"Congratulations!" Rhonda praised him. Turning back to Sage, she continued, "by the way, please excuse my poor manners. This is Sage Claremont. She's also a writer. We're publishing her first novel, and she's in town doing revisions."

"Great!" Roger shook Sage's hand enthusiastically. "May I join you ladies?"

"Of course," Rhonda motioned to an empty chair.

It was nearly midnight when Rhonda dropped Sage off back at her apartment building. She walked to the elevator slowly, making an effort to appear even on her feet. She didn't want Rhonda to know how tipsy she was! Rhonda waited in her car by the curb until Sage was safely inside the elevator before driving away. When the elevator doors closed, Sage sagged against the back wall and giggled as she thought about the evening. What fun! Spending an evening dining in a trendy pub while discussing books with another writer and her very own editor, was something that would never happen to her in Hope. As she drifted off to sleep, Sage briefly wondered what Cade was doing? I'm sure he's asleep by now, she thought as her mind went blank.

*   *   *   *

Buzzing June bugs and the rattle of the cottonwood's leaves in the night breeze seemed a cacophony to Cade as he tossed and turned in his bed, unable to sleep. His calls to Sage earlier in the evening, and even a couple of not-so-early attempts, yielded no answers. Where had she been? His mind raced with scenarios; none of them comforting. Sheer exhaustion finally overcame his worry, and he fell into a restless slumber sometime in the darkest hours of night.

*   *   *   *

Sage woke with a bleary head. Her first thoughts were of Cade, and she reached across the nightstand by her bed, fumbling for her cell phone. Two missed calls! Damn it! And both were from Cade. The only night she had done anything here, and he had finally called. Oh well, she thought, at least I know he's okay. Pushing the two button for Cade's speed dial setting, then hitting send, Sage waited for the familiar ringing. Her stomach jumped into her throat when his voice, velvety with sleep, uttered a delicious "hello."

"Cade?" she asked, although she knew it was him, knew the chocolaty timbre of his voice that vibrated down her spine.

"Hi Baby," he whispered. "How did you know I needed you?"

"I just knew, cowboy," Sage felt the arousal in her own voice. "Cause I need you the same way." She heard a soft, masculine moan, and knew that if she were there, if she reached beneath the sheet and ran her hand down taut belly, traced the vee of dark, curly hair down to the place it began to spread out again, her fingers would meet with the heat and hardness that evidenced his need.

"I've been trying to call you," her voice trailed off, but he could hear the question.

"Long hours," he assured her. "I want to surprise you with all the improvements. I tried to call you last night," he continued. "Late night?"

"Yes," she explained, trying not to sound guilty. After all, she hadn't done anything wrong. "Rhonda took me out for dinner. We ended up staying for drinks and talking with another writer that Heart represents. It was great!" The enthusiasm increased in Sage's voice as the memories of the previous night came back.

"That's nice, Hon," Cade assured her, although he wasn't at all sure he really meant it. "How are your revisions coming?"

"Good." She updated him on the recent suggestions and changes, "but I'll still have a lot to do when I get home. A lot of what I'm doing here is taking notes. I'll have to do the major re-write when I get back."

"I know," he admitted. "But I'll still be glad to have you back here. It's awfully lonely without you."

"I miss you too," Sage reassured him. "And I can't wait to be home, but I really do like it here. I definitely want to come back again." Her voice grew softer, "Maybe you could come with me next time?"

"Maybe," he half-heartedly agreed, "but it'll be hard to get away from the ranch for any length of time."

The lack of interest and enthusiasm in his voice halted Sage's excitement.

"Well, guess I better get ready for another day of revisions," she ended the conversation abruptly. "Bye Cade."

"Sage?" he began just as he heard the phone disconnect.

The next couple of days were busy ones for Sage, as the team worked with her to get through her manuscript by week's end. Her ticket home was for Saturday. She fell into her bed each night exhausted from the intense work. Her phone didn't ring, and she never tried to call Cade. She was tired of him ruining her excitement and her dreams. She rose early Saturday morning to get packed. Her flight was at 10:40, and Heart was sending a car at 8:30 to take her to the airport. Just as she stepped from the shower, the tune of her cell phone ringing caught her attention. She ran, dripping, to the bedroom trying to wrap a towel around her head as she went. She grabbed the phone just as it stopped ringing, then heard the beep of a message being left. She saw on her caller ID that it was her father. Pressing her PIN number into her voice mailbox, Sage waited for her Dad's familiar voice.

"Sage," he began, "this is Dad." His voice sounded worried. "Grandma had another heart attack early this morning. One of the nursing staff found her after she pushed her call button." He paused. "Give me a call when you get this, honey. Bye."

Sage collapsed on the bed, trembling. Grandma Nina! Please God, let her be okay! She quickly dialed her father's number.

"Dad?" Her voice wavered. "Is Grandma okay?"

"She's not good," his voice deepened with worry. "Doctor Rommel thinks her stint may have failed. The tests show that her heart has been severely damaged. Your mom and I are on our way to Hope right now. We'll be there in about half an hour."

"What does that mean, Dad, severely damaged?" Sage probed for more information.

"I'm not sure honey," Don Claremont could hear the panic in his daughter's voice. He had dreaded calling her. She and her grandmother were so close. "When we have more details, we'll call right away."

Sage explained her flight information to him, and then hung up. Her mind raced as she threw on clothes and crammed her belongings into her suitcases. She drug her things to the elevator, rode down, and pulled them out to the sidewalk just as her car pulled up. The driver, a taciturn man with short brown hair and a clean-shaven face, placed her luggage into the trunk, then opened the back passenger door for her, saying only "Madam?"

Sage climbed into the car and let her mind focus inward. When they arrived at La Guardia, Sage realized she couldn't remember anything about the drive. Her thoughts continued to be with Grandma Nina as she checked her bags and walked to her gate. The ringing of her cell phone startled her as she stared out the window waiting to board her plane.

"Hello?" Her voice sounded frantic, even to her own ears.

"Sage?" Her mother's voice somehow comforted her.

"What's happening? Are you there? How's Grandma?" Sage fired questions nervously.

"We're here, sweetie," Renee Claremont's voice sounded calm. Sage knew her Mom could always keep a level head in a crisis, so she wasn't completely reassured. "Your Dad is with Nina right now. She's sleeping. Dr. Rommel says they've given her medicine to stop the damage to her heart, and to help with the discomfort. The drugs will make her sleep. They want to send her back to Denver, but right now she isn't stable enough to make the trip."

"What does Dr. Rommel say?" Sage sounded desperate. She was desperate, desperate for someone to tell her that Grandma Nina would be okay, that she was going to make it.

"She says that all we can do it wait. In a few hours we'll know more. The damage is bad. Your Dad told you that, right?" Renee prompted her daughter.

"Yeah, he told me." Sage confirmed sadly.

"Did you know that Nina has a DNR order signed?"

"What's that?"

"It's short for Do Not Resuscitate. It means she doesn't want extreme measures taken to keep her alive."

Sage's heart fell.

"That sounds like Grandma," she admitted. "I guess we just never talked about things like that."

"You know she wouldn't want to be kept alive on machines."

"I know," Sage agreed.

"I just don't want to lose her." Tears ran down Sages cheeks, and Renee heard the anguish in her daughter's voice.

"None of us do," she empathized. "It's in God's hands now," she tried to reassure Sage. "All we can do is wait and pray."

Sage's flight home was interminable. Not being able to phone her parents and check on Grandma Nina's status was torture. When her plane finally touched down in Denver 2 1/2 hours later, Sage had her phone in hand and was ready to turn it on as soon as she was allowed. Her Dad answered, and told Sage that nothing had changed.

"How are you going to get here honey?" Don asked. "I was so worried about Mom that I didn't even think about not being there to pick you up."

"Don't worry," Sage assured him. "I'll just rent a car and drive out."

CHAPTER TWENTY-SEVEN

Sage went through the motions of collecting her bags and renting a car, but her mind was in Hope with her Grandma Nina. She breathed a sigh of relief when she finally left the traffic of Denver and the huge airport behind her, and headed east across the plains. The splendor of the Rocky Mountains loomed in her rear-view mirror, but she was too worried to appreciate their beauty. The long drive seemed even longer than usual, the grassy expanse of wide, rolling hills went on endlessly. Sage called her Dad's cell phone, and learned only that Grandma was resting before she went down a hill and lost the signal.

"Damnit!" she muttered, tossing her phone onto the passenger seat. Cell phone coverage was horrible out here, as always, Sage reminded herself. During her one of her two quick pit stops, she phoned Cade, and was relieved to hear him pick up.

"Hi sweetie," he answered.

"How did you know it was me?" she queried. "Or is that your typical phone greeting?" Despite her teasing tone, he heard the worry in her voice.

"Is everything ok?"

"No it isn't," she confessed. "Dad called me this morning just as I was leaving New York, and Grandma had another heart attack last night. She's resting right now, but the doctor said her prognosis isn't good."

"Oh baby, I'm so sorry." Cade's voice soothed her and she felt some of the tension leaving her body. Just having him there to hear her worries was a big relief.

"I'm so glad I got you." Her voice broke, and she began to cry softly. She leaned her head against the steering wheel as the tears flowed. Cade's heart nearly broke just hearing her grief.

"I'm leaving now, babe. I'll meet you there as quick as I can," The quiet strength in his voice calmed her.

"I love you so much," she hiccupped.

"I love you, too. Now hang up, take a deep breath, and get back on the road," he directed. "I'll see you in a few hours."

"Thank you," she whispered.

"That's what I'm here for. Bye sweet girl."

*　　　　*　　　　*　　　　*　　　　*

Cade threw a change of clothes into his old duffel, grabbed a cola from the fridge and headed for his truck. He wound his way along the now-familiar gravel road into town, and after a quick fuel stop, he was on the road toward Hope and the woman he loved. He couldn't wait to see her! He was so glad she was coming home, although he wished it were under better circumstances. He knew she was incredibly close to her Grandmother, and he realized how devastated she was over Nina's condition.. He wanted to talk to her more about her week in the Big Apple, too. He'd been aware of the tension between them during some of their phone conversations that week, and wanted to clear the air. To be honest, her excitement over the "city experience" had frightened him a bit. He hated to admit it, even to himself, but she meant the world to him now, and the idea that she might decide she liked the glamour of city life more than him had him scared spitless. Taking a deep breath, he turned up the radio and began to sing along to James Taylor as his old truck ate up the miles.

*   *   *   *
*

As Sage neared her home town, the familiar landmarks comforted her. The landscape changed, and more trees lined the little creeks than ran lazily among the rolling hills of pastureland. The giant cottonwoods spread their branches to provide huge circles of shade, and here and there a thicket of chokecherry bushes or plums grew along a fence line. She pulled into Hope about five p.m., and drove straight to the hospital. She recognized her parent's car parked in front, and pulled into a space one car over. She crawled slowly from the car, feeling stiff and sore from her long drive and the tension of worrying. Sage grabbed her purse, and walked toward the hospital entrance, dreading what she would find.

The automatic doors opened with a swish, and Sage inhaled the air that poured out of the opening. The scent of industrial cleaning products only slightly covered the less pleasant odors they were meant to take away. Sage strode past the nurse's station and glanced at the room numbers on the signs pointing down each of the two hallways in the little, rural hospital. Grandma Nina was in room 121, the same room she had been assigned during her previous stay.

Don and Renee Claremont both turned toward the door as Sage stepped into the room.

"Oh sweetie," Renee moved forward and wrapped her arms around Sage. They moved toward the bed together.

"It feels so peaceful in here," Sage's surprise was evident in her voice.

"Yes," Don spoke up. "It was the same when my Dad was dying."

"Dying. That sounds so awful!" Sage exclaimed.

"It really isn't," Renee's voice had a comforting tone. "Grandma had a long, fulfilling life. I know it's hard to let her go, but her heart is worn out now."

"I know," Sage admitted, "but I'll miss her so much!"

"We all will," Don agreed.

Cade observed the Claremonts as they said good bye to their much-loved mother and grandmother. It seemed he had spent much of his life losing the people he cared about. He knew that no matter how much it hurt at the time, you put one foot in front of the other and moved on with your life. The missing never went away, but there was room in your heart for new love, as he had recently learned.

The morning passed slowly as Grandma Nina's body slowed and then stopped. The heart monitor measured the final minutes of her life with beeps whose intervals lengthened until they were no more, and the monitor's screen showed a flat, green line that marked the end of a special life. Sage sat next to her grandmother's bed and held the older woman's hand until her shallow breathing stopped. They all cried; even Cade, who was surprised to feel tears streaming down his face; and then they walked arm in arm from the hospital.

*   *   *   *
*   *

The next week was a blur as funeral arrangements were made and the service was held. Grandma Nina was buried in the family plot next to Henry, her one true love. Sage helped her parents pack up grandma's belongings. She chose a few special pieces for herself; a collection of crystal and ceramic vases to hold the flowers from her grandmother's garden; the old manual typewriter that Nina had used during her years as a teacher and for her own personal writing; and the worn gardening gloves that Nina brought when she came to Sage's each Sunday for lunch and to help in the yard.

CHAPTER TWENTY-EIGHT

Cade stayed in Hope for a few days after the funeral. Sage was comforted by her regular routine, and with a sale coming up, began to cook and prepare for the café to be open. Ellie had done a great job running the café while Sage was gone, and Sage had been so grateful to have someone take over that she could count on to do it right. Cade stood in the kitchen, nursing a cup of coffee, and watching Sage roll out pie crusts.

"So, is it good to be back to your usual, or do you miss the city lights?" His comment sounded light-hearted, but his eyes held a serious look.

"Both, really," she glanced up from her task. "It feels comfortable to be home, and running the café isn't a bad gig, but I really loved the work I did in New York. Writing is my dream; it's the work I'm passionate about. The café is kind of a stopgap until I can make it with my writing."

"Is it the writing or the city that you loved most while you were there?" She could hear the fear in his voice. She knew what he wanted her to say, and to be honest she could say it truthfully.

"It's the writing. The city is great, but it's a place I love visiting. I don't want to live there. I have to admit, it was a real dream-come-true to be there at a publishing company working on my book with a real editor.

"I don't want to leave you, but I gotta get back to the ranch. One of my neighbors is taking care of Buck, and I've got so much still to do."

"I know," she continued rolling the supple dough. "I don't want you to leave either, but you've got your place now."

"I want it to be your place too."

"What are you saying Cade?" she whispered.

He set his coffee cup on the counter and stepped behind here. He slid his arms around her waist and hugged her, burying his face in her thick strawberry blonde hair.

"Please marry me, Sage?" He spoke softly, "Make my life perfect."

"Really? Oh Cade!" she exclaimed, turning to face him.

"The idea of going back to my place without you, without it being your place too, takes all the happiness out of it."

With tears streaming down her face, she looked up at him.

"I'd be honored to marry you! My answer is yes!"

The End